Only In My Dreams

A simple love story
Adapted from the novel "Into Each Life"

Shelia E. Bell

Only In My Dreams

A simple love story
Adapted from the novel "Into Each Life"

Shelia E. Bell

ISBN: 978-0-9838935-9-2

Library of Congress Control Number 2015918419

Bonita And Hodge Publishing Group
bandhpublishing@gmail.com

Acknowledgements

First and foremost, thank you God for your unlimited blessings, unconditional love, for your protection, and especially for your forgiveness. Thank you for blessing me with the love of family and friends, for giving me my own unique and special gifts and talents. Thank you for never leaving my side and for blessing my mind to write the stories that I write and guiding my hands to put take them from my mind and put them down from pen to paper.

Thank you to all of the readers who support my work, whether this is the first of my books that you have read or whether you are a loyal follower. You help to make me successful and enable me to live my dreams now. I appreciate you and I feel so grateful for you. May God bless you, keep you and forever be with you.

Shelia E. Bell

To those who are in love, to those who want to be in love, and to those who believe in love.

"If he's *only in my dreams,* don't wake me up, let me sleep." Shelia E. Bell

Ruth did not want to give Fantasia the impression that in order to be happy she had to have a man in her life. That was far from the truth. But she did want each of her children to experience the kind of love she had found with their father, Solumun, before his death.

Fantasia was well aware that her mother was concerned about her lack of romantic involvement. She was always the bridesmaid never the bride which suited her just fine. She'd had many an opportunity from many a man, but none could sway her to give up her heart for the sake of love. And contrary to rumors that circulated in the tabloids from time to time, she was not gay. She was, however, determined not to allow love to destroy her life as it had her mother.

"Fantasia, sweetheart, are you going out this evening?"

"No, Mama, I have a ton of paperwork I need to catch up, plus there's a sketch I want to work on. Tonight's the perfect time to do it."

"Fantasia, for goodness sakes, it's the weekend. Can't you find something better to do?"

"You mean *someone* better to do, don't you. But look, let's not go there. I don't have a date and I don't want one. How many times do I have to tell you that I'm happy with things just like they are?"

"I don't want to argue. I just hate to see you working all the time. Life's too short not to enjoy it."

"That's where you're wrong. I am enjoying my life. You don't seem to think so, but I am. You equate loving someone with being fulfilled and happy."

"That's not true, I never said that." Ruth didn't want to upset Fantasia but the tone of her voice told her it was too late. "I understand what you're saying. Everything is not going to be a bed of roses in life, Fantasia; I never said that it was."

"A bed of roses, it certainly is not, because life is a game, Mama. You just have to know how to play it. The God you worship seems to be the one who is the orchestrator of it all, including your no nonsense view on love. But answer this, what kind of love takes a daddy away from his children, Mama?"

"Oh, please, Fantasia. Don't be mean." Ruth started tearing up.

"Tell me, Mother. Don't start crying now. "Why does God allow the things He does? And you say that you want me to fall in love?"

Ruth stared into her daughter's cold and callous black eyes. Fantasia was the oldest child of three. Ever since her daddy's death when she was just a child, Fantasia had turned her back on God. As she grew older, she swore never to give her heart to a man.

Fantasia could see the hurt look on her mother's face, but she had to make Ruth understand once and for all that she had her life in order.

"Sorry, Mama. I don't mean to hurt you but I'm sick and tired of being made to feel like I'm wrong for not wanting a man in my life or God for that matter. I don't see the sense in any of it. So what does it matter? God does what he wants to do and I'm going to do what I want to do, live my life the way I want to. I'll help others when I can but forget that whole happily ever after farce."

Ruth wiped a tear from her cheek before she whisked around and rushed to the sanctity of her office.

Fantasia stood watching her until she disappeared. She replaced what had just happened with the task before her. Returning to her office, and taking a seat behind the walnut desk, she kicked off her heels and proceeded to leaf through the pile of neatly stacked papers.

Ruth fell back in the arms of the plush office chair. When she saw the box of tissues resting on the end table, she quickly grabbed one to wipe away her tears and clean her runny nose. She allowed her perfectly coiffed hair to lean against the high back of the chair. She needed answers before she could dish out any more advice.

Present

"We don't see things the way they are. We see them the way WE are." Talmud

"You are the most beautiful woman on earth. I love you more than life itself," he said. I want to spend the rest of my life with you." Fantasia couldn't contain the love she felt for the tall, dark, handsome man who was making love to her. Her life was perfect. She had everything a girl could wish for. The love of family, friends, a successful career, plenty of money and the perfect man, but there was one thing about him...he didn't exist in her reality.

Fantasia woke up, thinking about the dream that she had about the perfect guy. She'd been having the same dream on and off for the past few months, and she didn't know why. She raised up in her bed, smiled at the thought, pushed the dream aside, and then proceeded to get up and get ready for the busy day ahead.

♥

Fantasia Runsome sat in her lavishly furnished home office. Her determination, strong work ethics, and do or die zest to succeed had definitely paid off. Holding her Nero sketching pencil in hand, she looked around her office and admired her many accomplishments in the world of art. Her studio, Trinity Three Gallery and Museum, was doing far beyond well, but there still remained a thirst that was not quenched by all of the prestige, notoriety, and not to mention boatloads of cash that poured in from her world famous art pieces that were reserved for the rich and famous, such as herself. She'd proven many times over that she was a winner. Nothing in life was going to stop her.

Memories of her father's love, but worse her father's death, when she was a child, somehow were the force that propelled her forward. God had taken his life, stolen his future, and left her a bitter woman who didn't believe that love was possible.

She entertained these dreadful thoughts and mixed it with some reminiscing about how far she'd come in her thirty-five years on earth. She wasn't in her spacious home in Belleaf, Maryland. She'd chosen her sunny California vacation home to spend some much needed down time with her best friend and cousin, Paula.

Ruth, along with the staff of fifteen, could hold down the fort at Trinity Three while she spent some time away.

Paula barged into Fantasia's study, bringing a halt to her private thoughts.

"I'm going for a dip in the pool. You coming?" asked Paula.

"Umm, I don't think so. Why don't you go ahead. I have some phone calls to make and a few other things to finish up. I'll join you later."

"Look, girl, you have not pulled me away from my man and children to come out here with you only for me to be walking around this gigantic mausoleum by myself," complained Paula.

"First of all, this is not a mausoleum; it's my home away from home. Second, it should take me no more than an hour to finish up some loose business ends," responded Fantasia.

"Who do you think you're fooling? This is no vacation for you. All you ever do is work, work, and work. I don't understand you. You need some excitement in your life."

Fantasia whipped around in her chair. "Excitement? My life is an adventure as it is. I mean how much more exciting can it be? I travel wherever and practically whenever I choose. I'm surrounded by my world of art, which you know is my life; and I have a best friend not to mention cousin who loves to hang with me." Fantasia laughed.

"Don't try to get me with that best friend and cousin line. This best friend of yours has a life back home in Broknfield, Oregon. Thank God, Nick isn't one of those clingy, jealous types."

"That's because he knows I won't let you get into anything you shouldn't," mouthed Fantasia. "My opinion, not that you care, is men are nothing but trouble. There are a few exceptions, I must admit. Moses is a good man and husband to my mother; and Nick is a good husband and father to you and the kids. Ummm." Fantasia placed a finger to her lips. "I think that's it."

"I can't wait until your man comes sailing in here, swoops you off your feet, and shows you what love really has to do with it." Paula laughed and so did Fantasia.

"Will you get out of here so I can get done? I'll join you by the pool shortly. I promise."

"Yeah, whatever." Paula turned to leave.

"Oh, Paula, will you stop by the kitchen, if you don't mind, and ask Bianca to make us a pitcher of lemonade. Tell her to place it out by the pool."

"Sure. I'll see you in a few. But if you aren't out there in your teeny weenie, itsy bitsy bikini in less than an hour, I'm coming right back in here and pulling you away from that desk. I came out here to have some fun." Paula swished around and pranced out of the office. Her multi-colored, one-piece, halter top swimsuit was perfect for her thick, proportioned figure.

"I hear what you're saying. And I told you, I'll be out there before you know it."

Fantasia followed up with an extended Skype conversation with her commercial realtor in Broknfield who she'd been talking to the past few months. She hadn't revealed her potential expansion plans to anyone but her mother. She was still going over some demographic studies, the perfect location for a high end art studio, and other business notes with the hopes of opening her first gallery in her hometown of Broknfield.

"Sweet Taboo Art Gallery," she said as a broad smile of satisfaction appeared on her cherub like face. "I like that name. I like it a lot."

Fantasia finished her work and then hurried and changed into what must have been no more than a size six skimpy white bikini, and joined Paula at the pool.

Paula was sitting back comfortably in the chaise lounge chatting on her cell phone.

"How are the girls?" Fantasia heard her ask. "And how is my handsome, sexy hubby?"

"Girl, you can't talk about me. Look at you. I bet you've been on the phone with Nick every since you left my office."

Paula looked over her shoulder. The Bluetooth was visible in her ear. "I sure have. Oh, Nick said either you spend some quality time with me or he's coming down here this weekend and showing me some attention."

"Tell that husband of yours that he knows better than anybody how much time it takes to run a successful business. How many men's stores does he have now?" mocked Fantasia.

Paula repeated to Nick what Fantasia said. Fantasia walked over to the outside kitchen area and poured a tall glass of lemonade.

"Ahh, this is delicious," she said as she took a couple of swallows of the freshly squeezed lemonade. "Bianca makes the best lemonade I've ever tasted," she said to Paula as if Paula was not on the phone.

"Yeah, she does, doesn't she?" responded Paula. Her half full glass sat on the table next to her. "Nick says that he's serious about coming to LA this weekend. He and his business partner are thinking about opening an NT's Men's Store on Rodeo Drive. He wants to take a look at some spaces."

Fantasia sat in the chaise next to Paula. "No problem for me. He's your man. You're the one who has to give him your attention."

"I love you too," Paula said and made a smacking sound into her cell phone. "Bye, baby."

She turned and focused her attention on Fantasia. "You sure you don't mind if Nick comes?"

"Girl, how many times are you going to ask me that same question? When have I ever had a problem with Nick or the kids being here? You're the one who said you wanted to get away for a while. But if you like it, I love it." She sat her glass of lemonade on the round table next to her. "How is the water?"

"Fabulous," answered Paula.

Fantasia got up, went to the edge of the pool, and jumped in. She swam several laps before swimming back over to the edge and splashing water on Paula. "Come on in here. Don't hold back now that I'm out here."

Paula joined Fantasia in the pool. The women swam several laps, did some water aerobics for awhile and then stopped and sat on the steps of the pool to talk.

"Girl, tell me about the date you had the other day." Paula asked.

"There's nothing to tell. We had dinner at one of his restaurants. He's a great conversationist and definitely easy on the eyes." Fantasia giggled and so did Paula.

"Are you planning on seeing him again when you get back to Belleaf?"

"Don't know. We've talked a few times. But you know me; I don't have time for a love connection."

"You need to make time, Fantasia. You're not getting any younger. If you plan on doing the married with children thing, I suggest you get to moving, girlfriend."

"You're starting to sound like my mother."

"That's only because Aunt Ruth feels the same way I do. It's time for you to meet someone and fall in love. Have some little artists running through these empty mansions you have all over the United States."

"And why is that so necessary? I don't know if I want kids. Plus, Hope has enough children for me, you, and everybody else. Seven children, whew. How she does it, is beyond me. Who ever thought I'd have a sister with a basketball team of her own."

"I wonder why she wanted so many kids? I don't see how Hope does it. Seven kids and counting. Girl, added Paula, "Jenay and Talisa are enough for me."

"Yeah, I know right. I don't think she has plans on stopping either. She and David don't believe in practicing birth control. They believe that far-fetched mess about being fruitful and multiplying." Fantasia climbed out of the pool. "I love my brother-in-law, don't get me wrong. And I respect the fact that he's a preacher and all, but keeping Hope barefoot and pregnant is so archaic."

"Yea, but there's nothing wrong with that if that's what they want to do. To each his own."

"Exactly, so don't be on me about a serious relationship. I'm perfectly happy just the way things are. You know I've never been one to fall for the lovey dovey stuff. I keep telling everybody that love is for the weak. And, if I did happen to meet someone that I think deserves my time and attention, I don't have to marry him to have children. I don't need a husband in order to have a family. If I wanted to I could buy myself a sperm donor. I'm not going to be left crying and hurting for years and years like my mother did after my daddy died."

"I feel sorry for you."

"I don't know why you feel sorry for me. I'm good."

"I'm just saying, we were kids when Uncle Solumun died. No one could do anything about that. He had an aneurysm. That was nobody's fault. It was God's will."

Fantasia got out of the pool and walked over to where she left her glass of lemonade. She removed its rubber lid, took a swallow, then laid back against the chaise lounge.

Paula climbed out of the pool right behind her. Grabbing hold to her beach towel, she dried her hair and body, and then sat down.

Fantasia watched Paula take a seat on the chaise. "God's will, umph."

"I'm not going to ruin our time together by getting in a disagreement with you about God. It's obvious to everyone who knows you, well anyone in the family, that you and God are not on the best of terms."

"You have it all wrong."

Paula's expression changed from concern to excitement. "What? You mean you don't feel that way anymore?"

"No, that's not what I mean. I have everything a person could want. I'm successful and I'm rich. I'm doing what I love to do. Everything is at my fingertips. What do I need God or a man for? My father trusted in God most of his life. I remember him being the kind of man that taught us to put God first in everything we did. We had to go to church like twenty four seven." Fantasia smiled slightly. "Seems like everywhere you looked in our house back then had something to do with God. What did all of his belief and trust get him? A death sentence. So, let's not even go there."

"I don't understand you. How can you not believe in God? It just doesn't make sense. Look up at the sky. Look at the water in the pool. Look at the trees. Girl, look all around you. It's obvious that God exists."

"You know me well enough to know that I don't fall for any of your religiosity. You and your family hang out at church like it's your second home. You say you don't see how I don't fall for all of that, and I say that I don't see why you *do* fall for it. Think about it, how can you say there is a God? What makes you so sure?"

"What makes me so sure is the very fact that I am sitting here breathing, moving, and talking. I am not my own. I believe in what the Word of God says."

"Paula, you are so naïve. There is no way you, me, or anyone can know for sure that there is some super, sovereign being called God. You cannot sit here and tell me that you know how the universe was really created. There are thousands of religions all over the world. And you want me to trust in this God of my father and you? No way." Fantasia shook her head from side to side. "Not this chick. I'm doing just fine the way things are. Hey, how did we get on this subject anyway? I thought you wanted to know about the restaurateur who wined and dined me."

"You're right. I don't feel like arguing with you. So, tell me about him. But before you do, let me say this one more time. It's not like I haven't told you a zillion times already. But God loves you."

"Yea, yea, yea. Ewww, you sound like Hope. But don't let me talk her up. She'll call me and start going through her witnessing ritual. One thing about Hope and David, they know they don't give up on what they believe. They'll try to make you choke on it if that's what they think it takes." Fantasia took another swallow of lemonade. "Now." She cleared her throat before continuing. "Mr. Restaurateur was the perfect gentleman. We had a five course meal that was to die for, Paula. The man showered me with the most gorgeous flowers and he scored extra brownie points when I saw several pieces of my artwork lining the walls of his restaurant. The man has exquisite taste."

"So you like him?"

"Of course I like him. He's sweet."

"Does he have a real name?"

"Yes. But I'm not telling. Mum's the word."

"But I thought I was your best friend," Paula said in a whining tone.

"You are, but he isn't going to be around long enough, so there's no need to tell you who he is." Paula threw up her hand. "Whatever, girl. But anyway, will you at least agree to be cordial to Nick's new business partner when they come? His name is Randall Hughes, and I'm telling you, he's a pretty nice guy. Never been married, no girlfriend...or boyfriend, at least not that I know about." Paula and Fantasia laughed. "He has no children and he's quite successful. His parents died a few years ago. From what Nick says, they left him a big chunk of money."

"I'll think about it. You don't know if Nick is coming to LA for sure. Once he lets you know, then we'll go from there."

"You are one tough cookie. I think you were cut from your own personal cookie cutter mold."

"Definitely," answered Fantasia. "Definitely."

2

"You know you're in love when you can't fall asleep because reality is finally better than your dreams." Dr. Seuss

"Please, be on your best behavior, Fantasia," Paula pleaded.

"Look, I am not one of your children. I do not need you to tell me how to act or react to this character Nick is bringing with him."

"I know, I know," Paula replied. "But I know you all too well. All I'm asking is for you to give Randall a chance."

"I had Bianca to make sure his room is ready. I *should* make the brotha stay at a hotel."

Paula let out a long audible breath. "Oh, no you wouldn't do that."

"Since you know me so well, you should know I would do it in a heartbeat." Fantasia snapped her fingers. "But don't worry; I'll be hospitable as long as he doesn't have any preconceived notions of coming here for a booty call."

"Fantasia, you are something else. Just be cool for once and let's have a good time this weekend. Nick and Randall will be gone most of Saturday looking for some prospective places for the store."

"What time are you supposed to pick up Nick and this partner of his?" questioned Fantasia.

"Their flight comes in at seven fifteen this evening. But I don't have to pick them up. They're renting a car."

"Would you like me to have the staff to prepare dinner for the four of us?"

"Would you do that?" Paula looked at Fantasia with pleasure glistening in her eyes.

"Of course. The least I can do is feed them, especially before I send Randall off to a hotel." Fantasia's head went backward as a burst of laughter poured from her mouth.

Paula reached for one of the throw pillows off of Fantasia's sofa and threw it at her. It missed. "Don't you dare," she said.

"Girl, do you have any idea how much that pillow cost?"

"Nope. But I do know that you are one vain best friend. A pillow can be replaced. It's true love that's priceless."

"Glad I'm not in want of it," remarked Fantasia. "Come on, let's go in the kitchen and see what the chef suggests for dinner."

♥

The four of them sat around a dining room table that was laid out for royalty. From the exquisite, stunning pattern of Syracuse place settings down to the salad bowl, everything was picture perfect.

"Fantasia, thank you for extending your hospitality toward me," Randall told her. He took a bite of his appetizer. "My compliments to the chef. This is delicious." Randall sunk his fork into another one of the baseball sized meatballs. "May I ask the name of it?"

"It's one of my favorites. They're truffles made of Gouda cheese and grits, stuffed with crabmeat and drizzled with an avocado-based sauce. When I was attending an art show in the south a couple of years ago, I was taken to a restaurant and when I saw these on the menu, I had to try them. After that, I was hooked," Fantasia said with a smile on her face. "I asked my chef to recreate it, and he always does a marvelous job."

"I agree," said Randall.

"It is good," added Paula.

"Yeah, very," commented Nick as he stuck a bite-sized portion into his mouth.

After they dined on the main course of beef wellington, green beans with lemon sauce and brown rice, accompanied by their choices of red or white wine, the four of them went outside on the lanai and enjoyed the amazing California view.

"Fantasia, I can't thank you enough for the delicious meal," Nick told her.

"Anytime, Nick. It's been a while since I've seen you. How are things going with your stores? Paula says that you've come to LA to do some scouting for a new one."

"True. Randall just came on board with NT as Senior Vice President of Marketing. We've crunched numbers, checked demographics, and marketability, which led us here. I think it's time I expand my dream and open that men's boutique on Rodeo."

"Nothing to it but to do it. I believe in grabbing hold of the gusto of life as long as you can. I don't want to look back on life and regret having not done something that I always wanted to do," said Fantasia.

"I agree with you on that," Randall added.

Fantasia nodded.

"Honey, what time are you and Randall planning on going out tomorrow?"

"We plan on getting up early and hit the pavement running. That's why we decided to rent a car instead of catching a cab here. We plan on covering a lot of ground."

"If you need any help, let me know," offered Fantasia. "I have quite a few contacts that I can call on that will be more than willing to help you out."

"Wow, thanks for the offer, Fantasia. I might have to take you up on that," said Nick.

"Yeah, that sounds great," added Randall.

"I'm thinking about opening a gallery in Broknfield myself. Not on the scale of the one in Belleaf, but it's still going to be top of the line. I thought this one could offer art lessons to some of the high school students who show a promising future in the arts."

"Seriously? That sounds like a great idea."

"Yep. I think that sleepy town could use a little artistic makeover." Fantasia and her guests all laughed.

"Excuse me," said Nick as he yawned.

"You tired, baby?" asked Paula, rubbing Nick's back in a circular motion.

"Yeah, I am. It's been a long day."

"Why don't we go upstairs and get ready for bed? I'll call and check on the kids when we get to our room."

"Okay," said Nick. "I'm sure they're fine. Your mother will keep them under control."

"I know, but I still want to check on them." Paula glanced in Fantasia's direction and winked at her out of the eye view of Nick and Randall. "Thank you for dinner, Fantasia. I'll see you in the morning."

"Randall, I'll show you to your room if you're ready to call it a night," Fantasia told him.

"Thank you, but if you don't mind I'd like to sit out here under the stars and enjoy this spectacular night view just a little bit longer."

"Sure, no problem."

"Well, good night, guys," Fantasia said to Paula and Nick. "If you need anything, you can call Bianca. There's an intercom in your room."

"I don't think we'll need anything, but thanks anyway," said Nick.

"Nite, Fantasia," said Paula.

On his way inside the house, Nick stopped and leaned down to kiss Fantasia on her forehead.

"Randall, you straight?" Nick asked.

"Yeah, man. I'm straight."

Fantasia and Randall remained silent for several moments after Paula and Nick left.

Randall's clean cut features, mystical gray eyes, shaved head, and coffee brown skin enhanced his glistening smile and accentuated his baritone voice. "God's earth is truly amazing," he said and gazed upward.

"I don't know about it being God's earth, but I do agree that the world is a beautiful place," said Fantasia. "That's one of the reasons I love art. Art expresses the deepest, most intimate, most astonishing features of the world, people, animals, simply everything. It can all be found in some form of art."

Randall turned from looking at the sky and focused on Fantasia.

"What?" she asked when she saw him look at her without saying anything.

"I was just thinking."

"Thinking about what?" she asked.

"That you're a piece of art yourself."

"Man, please. Is that your best pick up line," remarked Fantasia.

Randall's eyebrows rose. "Pick up line? I'm sorry, but I was being complimentary. I don't want to sound disrespectful, but the fact is I wasn't flirting with you."

Fantasia's eyes widened. "Good, because I know Paula. She has a tendency to play millionaire matchmaker. But to set the record straight, I'm not interested. I can get a man without anyone's help."

"Whew, that's a relief," remarked Randall.

"Relief? What do you mean?"

"Because Nick calls himself fixing me up with you. Why? I can't tell you that, because like you, I've never had a problem getting a girl."

"This is so funny."

"I must confess. I didn't like the idea, but what could I say? I mean we made plans to come to Cali. So I gave in."

"I know. Paula used somewhat the same excuse."

"But I want to be honest with you from the jump."

"Good, I like a man who's honest," Fantasia said.

"You seem nice, but," he paused. "Let me just leave it at that." He shifted the subject. "You have a nice layout here. Relaxing and luxurious. You have excellent taste."

"Uhh, thank you. But don't try to spare my feelings. Go on and say what's on your mind," she insisted. "Believe me, I don't ruffle easily." She broke into a smile.

"It's just that, well, people like you, I mean, look at all of this," he said and looked from side to side at the splendor of Fantasia's home. "You're obviously a blessed woman, but you act like you did all of this on your own."

Fantasia sat up straight with an extra stiffness in her back. Who was he to be judging her? "Excuse me? What are you talking about?"

"I mean, you have it going on, as you put it. To look at you, you have it made. Lots of money, this place. People waiting on you hand and foot."

"Do I detect a bit of jealousy, Randall?"

"Definitely not. It's just that people like you amaze me. You think you're some self-made woman?" Randall shook his head.

"Who do you think you are?" she huffed. "And what do you mean by people like me? Are you talking about people like me who have put in their time, paid their dues, and earned every penny I have? Sounds to me that you are definitely envious of my success, Mr. Randall Hughes," she scoffed then slowly rose from her chair. She was more than irritated with this guy who'd come up in her house, ate her food, was enjoying her layout, and now he wanted to take digs at her? How dare he?

"Look, men like you are so typical. You can't handle it when a woman has more than you. You get all uptight and intimidated. Well, let me remind you of something." From where she stood, she pointed an accusatory finger toward him. "You and me," she pointed at herself, "have nothing in common. You could never be anything to me, not even a hit and run."

"You still don't get it." He drew his lips in thoughtfully. "You're so lost, so wrapped up in all of your material wealth. You don't realize that all of this stuff can be gone in an instant. Don't you understand that it's God who has blessed you with wealth and fame?"

"Ohhh, so that's what this is about? A sermon? Man, get a life. I don't have time for this." She waved her hand and proceeded to walk toward the entrance into the house.

"Go on. Run. That's probably something you're used to doing."

Fantasia didn't know how to react to Randall's searing words. She was the one who always had the upper hand, especially when it came to men. But suddenly she felt insecure and uncertain. She cleared her throat. "Look, I don't have time to listen to this pettiness you're talking about. But I will tell you this one thing," she said placing one hand on her hip and looking back over her shoulder at Randall, "If you weren't Nick's business partner, you'd be out of here in a split second. But then again, I'm bigger than that. I won't give a wannabe like you the time of day.... or night. Now, if you'll excuse me, I'm going to my room."

"Enjoy your night," Randall said in a smooth, even tone, not showing the least sign of discontent or annoyance at Fantasia's cutting remarks.

"Oh and please, feel free to enjoy the pool, or any of the other amenities. There's a full gym on the left wing of the house, plenty of food in the main kitchen and if there's something special you want prepared, all you have to do is use the intercom and one of the kitchen staff can whip you up something and bring it to your room," she said with biting sarcasm in her every word.

Randall came back with his own quick-on-his-feet response. "That's where you're wrong, sweetheart. I don't envy anything you have. Just the opposite. I'm proud to know about your accomplishments, and I appreciate your hospitality. I believe I'll take you up on the offer and go have a quick workout."

"Suit yourself. Good night," Fantasia said and walked away. *Uggg, the nerve of him. Talking about me while in the same breath, he's not turning anything down.*

♥

Fantasia tossed and turned in her oversized king canopied bed. Everything Randall said kept replaying in her mind. If Randall Hughes wanted to pretend like he wasn't fascinated by her, let him play that game. There wasn't a man she'd yet to meet who wasn't taken in by her success, and she couldn't see him being any different. He was just using another approach to try and get next to her. Well, it wasn't going to work. She was too smart to be caught up in a weak game like the one Randall was trying to play.

She sat up in her bed and looked around the massive suite. She got up, walked to the other side of her bedroom, through the sitting room, and into another hallway. She turned to the right and went into her office. She sat behind her desk, retrieved the folder labeled, "Sweet Taboo Art Gallery and Institute." She studied the files that her consultant had presented to her two weeks prior to her coming to California. His plans were well laid out and offered Fantasia a clear cut insight into how a place like Sweet Taboo might benefit the small town of Broknfield, Oregon which was comprised of mostly middle and lower income families. She wanted to give back to her childhood neighborhood in some way, so what better way than to show young, talented people the kind of life they could have through the world of art.

After going over the files for almost an hour, she put everything back where it belonged, neat and in order. She was a stickler for everything being in its proper place. She pressed the intercom in the bathroom. When Bianca answered, she told her that she was going to take a shower and asked her to come upstairs with her tea.

Under the powerful but soothing jet streams, Fantasia felt her body relax. It was better than being in a Jacuzzi. The warm water hit every area of her body, massaging her like a professional masseuse. After she finished and stepped out of the walk–in shower, big enough to fit at least six to eight people, Fantasia dried off and sat down in front of her vanity and began to groom her body. Upon entering her bedroom, she noticed that Bianca had changed her linen and turned back her bed.

Fantasia inhaled the lavender aroma filtering through her room. She laid on top of the welcoming Egyptian cotton bed linen. Her natural naked beauty was not covered by lingerie or pajamas. Fantasia loved the skin she was in and sleeping in what she arrived into the world in was what she loved to do. Whenever she was at the villa alone, she would often skinny dip in the pool. There was something invigorating and exciting about being free of clothing.

A cup of hot herbal tea sat next to the bed along with her nightly dose of Xanax. She only asked her doctor in Belleaf to prescribe her the pill to help alleviate some of the anxiety of her busy life. She saw nothing wrong with it, though her mother would beg to differ. Fantasia could hear her now. "Fantasia, you don't need to take drugs to sleep. You need to pray."

Fantasia dismissed the voice of her mother, popped the pill, drank her tea, and then pulled the cover up around her neck.

Randall worked up a sweat on the state of the art exercise equipment in Fantasia's weight room. After he finished lifting weights, and before he decided to call it a night, he went to the pool and swam a few laps. Later that evening, he retired to the guest room, took a shower, then perused some of the notes that he and Nick had prepared for their scouting venture.

Randall looked around. The room was fit for a king. A huge sitting area, linen covered lounge chairs, picture window, simply an oasis of peace and tranquility swathed in a sky blue color theme.

Randall retrieved his Bible from his luggage and prepared to locate the next on his quest to read the Bible in a year. So far, he had managed to stay on track with his daily readings. He read the appropriate s for the day and then climbed back out of the bed, got down on his knees and prayed. When he got back in the bed, he placed his hands behind his head and then smiled. "You are a piece of art," he said out loud as he looked around the opulent guest suite. "Fantasia, Fantasia Runsome. What has you so bitter and so angry at God...and men?"

He hadn't meant to come down on her as hard as he did, but he couldn't understand how people with her status and in her position could overlook being thankful to God. But then again, he ran across people like Fantasia everyday so there was no reason he should have been surprised. Even so, the fact remained that there was something about her that intrigued him. He wanted to learn more about her, but then he reminded himself that he was in Cali for nothing more than business. It didn't matter how much Nick and his wife wanted to play hook up for him, Fantasia could never be the cream in his cup of coffee. He had prayed and asked God for a mate, and he was not about to be caught up in Fantasia. Plus, unbeknownst to Nick and Paula, shortly before he met Nick, he and his girlfriend of two years had recently called off their engagement. Her job with a financial investment company had transferred her to Memphis and a long distance relationship proved that she wasn't the faithful girl he thought that she was. He had suspected some infidelity from the way she had been behaving a few months before they ended it all. When Randall discovered through a string of posts on Facebook that she was involved with another man, who happened to be her boss, it was the end of their relationship. The fact that she even admitted posting the comments on purpose hurt him, but now he had gotten over it. He thanked God that he found out that she wasn't ready to be a wife to him before they exchanged vows.

When it came to Fantasia, it didn't matter how beautiful, smart and successful she was, Fantasia Runsome was not the woman he was looking for either.

3

"Being single doesn't mean you don't know anything about love, it just means you know enough to wait for it." Unknown

"Girl, I don't know where that man came from, but I was two seconds from throwing him out on his face last night. He acted like he was my judge and jury." Fantasia explained the previous night's conversation between her and Randall to Paula.

"He's never come across as being the envious type, though. I mean, Randall is a really cool guy. I haven't known him that long, but the times I've been around him he just seems like a nice dude. He can get a little preachy at times because he's all into God," Paula said and raised her fingers in gesture. "But that's just the way he is. He's just serious about what he believes."

"I can respect that, but he sure doesn't respect mine. I mean, just because I don't walk around spouting scriptures and saying hallelujah, thank you, Jesus doesn't mean that I'm any less than he is. That's exactly why folks have problems with you people."

"I don't know what you're talking about. I'm not a 'you' people. You don't see me walking around like I'm all holier than thou. I believe what I believe but I certainly don't go around trying to push my beliefs off on the next person."

"Exactly. But dude wanted me to say that I have what I have because of God, and I just don't feel like that, Paula. And I won't apologize for it."

"Look," Paula said while placing an arm around Fantasia's shoulder. "I don't think he was trying to do that. I'm telling you, the man is super cool. You just have to get to know him. Stop being so uptight and defensive."

"Look, I don't want to get to know him, and I wish you and Nick wouldn't try to make something happen between us because it's not going to."

"Okay, okay." Paula raised both hands in surrender. "Forget Randall. Let's get ready to get out of here. You promised we were going to get our shop on. I want to go on Rodeo Drive."

"We haven't had breakfast yet and you're already talking about going shopping." Fantasia laughed.

"I sure am. I'm ready to have some fun."

Nick suddenly appeared in the outside dining area.

"Hey, I thought you and Randall had already left," said Paula.

"No, not yet," he answered then looked at Fantasia. "Hey, girl."

"Good morning, Nick."

"I hope you don't mind that I took advantage of your generosity and used your office to go over our plans for the day."

Fantasia shook her head. "Of course, I don't mind. By the way, where is your friend, business associate, or whatever?" Fantasia asked, almost snapping her neck like a valley girl.

"Why do you sound like that?" Nick asked.

"Like what? I just asked a simple question."

"She thinks Randall is too obsessed with religion," blurted Paula. "You know Randall, baby."

"Yeah, I do. Look, Fantasia, I know you don't like to get on a religious tip and all, but Randall is just like that. He doesn't mean any harm. He just wants to save the world. That's all," Nick said and smiled.

"I don't have a problem with him wanting to save the world. What I have a problem with is him trying to save *me* like I'm lost or something. Just because I don't sing to the same tune as he does doesn't make me less than him. Anyway, enough talk about Randall. Let me check to see what's taking so long for them to serve breakfast." Fantasia got up and walked toward the kitchen area.

"Yeah, now that's what I'm talking about," Nick commented, rubbing both hands together. "I'm starving," he said and smiled.

"You're always starving," chided Paula. "Fantasia, please hurry and get this man of mine something to eat."

"I'll be right back."

In her absence, Randall appeared.

"Good morning," Paula said as soon as his tall frame darted the door of the dining room.

"Good morning, Paula. What's up, Nick?"

"You got it, bro." Nick motioned for Randall to come further into the dining room. "Did you sleep all right?" Nick asked.

"Man, yeah. That's why I'm just making it down here. When I climbed up in the center of that bed last night, it was like somebody had drugged me because that's all she wrote. I was out for the count." Randall laughed.

"I'm glad you were comfortable," Fantasia said. Both men looked toward Fantasia like they'd been caught off guard with her sudden entrance. She walked into the dining area followed by Bianca and two other Hispanic males, one pushing a cart loaded with a variety of breakfast foods. The other male pushed a cart with an array of juices, water, tea and coffee.

"Breakfast is served," she said and the servers began to place several bowls and plates of food on the table. "Help yourselves."

"You don't have to tell me twice," Nick said. As soon as they finished plating the food, he mouthed a quick prayer then started serving himself eggs, bacon, sausage, biscuits, waffles and preserves.

"Nick, don't act like you don't have any home training. Fantasia, excuse my husband. I promise you he doesn't usually act like this." She and Fantasia both laughed.

"He's making himself at home and that's quite all right with me. I love for my guests to enjoy themselves." She looked over at Randall and cut her eyes.

"Umm," Randall said clearing his throat. "Everything looks delicious." He scooped some of the mixed fruit and put it on his plate. Like Nick, before he took his first bite, he closed his eyes, bowed his head and prayed to himself.

"Is that all you're having?" Paula asked.

"I'm just starting off small. I wouldn't want you two to think I was like my boy Nick over here." Randall back flipped his thumb in Nick's direction before chuckling.

"I'm just enjoying a good meal. I'm not worried about what you all are talking about," Nick commented and continued eating. "Honey," he said between a bite of his bacon. "You better fix yourself something. You said you and Fantasia were going out for the day. No need to start out on an empty stomach."

"I know." She proceeded to choose several items and put them on her plate.

"Paula, you all take your time. I'm going upstairs to get dressed."

"You aren't going to eat?" Nick asked and Paula looked up.

"No, I'm not a breakfast person. I'll eat something later. Excuse me," she said.

"You're excused," Randall replied. "Enjoy your day and thanks for the wonderful meal."

Fantasia turned and exited the room.

"Ouch," said Randall. "Don't know why that sister seems to have it in for me."

"Because you hurt her feelings, that's why," answered Paula.

"Yeah, man," added Nick. "You can't be going around forcing your beliefs down people's throats. You know not everybody wants to hear that kind of talk."

"That kind of talk? Bro, you know as well as I do that *that kind of talk* is needed in the world today. It's called witnessing." Looking at each of them, he said, "Paula...Nick, you already know that's how I roll. And I didn't think I said or did anything to hurt the lady's feelings."

"I'm just saying, we're here on business."

"Not me. I'm here to get my party on," Paula said jokingly and put another forkful of food in her mouth.

"You know what I mean," Nick said. "All I'm saying is there's a time and a place for everything."

Randall raised his eyebrows. "Sure, you're right. I'll apologize to her before we leave."

"That's straight," said Nick before turning his attention to his wife. "Baby, we'll probably be gone until late afternoon. We are going to cover as much ground as we can while we're here. You know we're out of here tomorrow morning."

"Yeah, I figured as much. Me and Fantasia will probably be gone just as long. I have a long list of things I want to do."

Nick shook his head. "Yeah, but yours involves spending money, and as for me, well let's just say I have to find ways to make the money so you can keep spending it."

Paula smiled, hunched her shoulders and kept eating without skipping a beat.

Randall laughed. "You guys are a trip. But I love it. You get along so well."

Paula looked at Nick and Nick returned her gaze. "Yep, I agree," she said.

Nick leaned over and kissed her on the lips before refocusing his eyes and appetite on his dwindling plate of food.

4

"Two people don't have to be together right now, in a month, or in a year. If those two people are meant to be, then they will be together somehow at some time in life." Unknown

"Fantasia is a true piece of work," Randall casually said as they drove to their first business meeting of the day.

"Yeah, she is," said Nick. "But like I told you, sometimes you have to go easy on the God talk. Not everybody wants to hear that, you know."

"I understand, but I didn't think I was preaching to her or anything like that. I was just laying some knowledge on her."

"Maybe she doesn't want to hear that kind of knowledge, bro." Nick steered the rental car on to the next street. "Fantasia is a cool chick. Why don't you try wining and dining her before you start preaching and teaching?"

Randall grinned. "You just might be on to something there. But I don't do long distance relationships. I know how those can turn out. We're headed back to Broknfield tomorrow, and she's a world traveler from what I hear you and Paula saying about her. I don't think she has time to put into a relationship, and I'm not out for some fly by night chick. I've had enough of those kinds of females. Plus, bottom line, she isn't my type. God has the perfect woman for me out there somewhere. And when she comes into my life, I'm sure I'll recognize her."

"I heard that. But you never know, man. Things happen when you least expect it and with whom you least expect them to." Nick shrugged. "So never say never."

They arrived at their first prospective location, talked with the commercial realtors, toured the space and then went on their way to their next destination.

♥

"Look at this dress," said Paula. "I love it. You can never find anything like this back in Brokenfield. Everything is way behind, especially fashion." Paula placed the dress against her and stood in front of the full-length mirror.

"Try it on," Fantasia suggested.

"Why?"

"What do you mean, why? You said you liked it. And we *are* shopping, aren't we?" remarked Fantasia. "I mean, I don't do the window shopping thing. If I see something I like, I get it."

"That's you. You have it like that. Me, I'm a dreamer. Even if it fits, I do not have," she looked at the tag again, "five hundred and fifty bucks. Oh my gosh," she squealed. She looked at another dress and the price tag on it made her eyes bulge. "Oh, yeah, I am definitely in the wrong store, girl. We need to go to TJ Maxx."

Fantasia motioned with her hand. "Girl, go on. Have a little fun. Try both of them on. It won't hurt you to dream a little."

"Dream, this is more than a dream; it's a fantasy," Paula said as she studied both of the dresses carefully. "Anyway, you said you don't do window shopping, and with these outrageous prices, that's all I'm going to be doing."

"Try...them...on," Fantasia insisted. "We're having fun. I think I'm going to try a couple on myself. I like this one. Look at it." She held up a sleeveless silk dress with a leather belt and a rounded neckline."

"Let me see that. It's cute. They must be crazy," Paula yelled. Looking embarrassed, she quickly scoped her surroundings as if to make sure no one heard her outburst. "Eight hundred and seventy-five dollars? For this?" she reduced her voice to a whisper.

Fantasia chuckled. "You have to pay for the best. Now, come on, let's try these on."

Fantasia walked to the sales associate who escorted them to a dressing room.

"Girl, this is huge," Paula said to Fantasia who was in the dressing room adjacent to hers. "I can live in here," she quipped.

"You are a nut. Will you stop making me laugh, and just try on your dress?"

"Okay, okay. But I'm just saying."

"So what's up with Nick's friend?" asked Fantasia as they simultaneously stepped outside their respective dressing rooms, and into the open area. "What do you think? How does it look on me?" Fantasia asked without waiting on Paula's response to her initial inquiry.

"I love it. It fits you perfectly. And that tangerine color really complements your skin tone. "But for what it costs, it should at least do that much."

Fantasia twirled around and studied herself in the wrap around mirror. "Look at you. Those mixed shades of blue do the same for you. Let's get them."

"Are you crazy?" Paula responded and started walking back toward the dressing room. "Nick would have a fit if I came back with something this expensive."

"You're out here to have fun. Part of having fun is splurging, spending money, doing the things you always wanted to do."

"No, having fun to me is window shopping and dreaming about all the things I want to do," Paula corrected.

"We are getting these dresses. It's on me."

"No, I can't let you do that."

"You're right. You can't, but I'm doing it anyway, because I want to. Call it an early birthday present."

"My birthday just passed, Fantasia, and you already got me something," Paula said and stepped into the dressing room to take off the dress.

"So it's an early uhhh, Christmas present," Fantasia said from her dressing room.

"I don't know what to say."

"Say nothing. Now get dressed. We still have a lot to do."

The ladies presented both dresses to the sales lady and Fantasia paid for them. After they left the store, and stepped outside into the welcoming sunlight, Paula stopped and hugged Fantasia.

"What was that for?"

"Thank you. Thank you so much. You've made my vacation the best ever, Fantasia. And please, please don't think I was looking for you to buy me anything. You're always so good to me, and I would never take advantage of your generosity."

"Girl, please. I know that. And you're welcome. Let's go to our next destination. How about we go on Rodeo Drive next?"

"Ooh, wee. Yes, yes, yes," Paula shrieked and they both climbed into Fantasia's luxury car.

"What was that you asked me back there?"

"What are you talking about?" asked Fantasia.

"You asked me something about Randall, didn't you?"

"Oh, yeah. It was nothing. I was just asking you what was up with him. He's a cutie, with those Michael Ealy eyes, but he's way too judgmental for my taste. If it wasn't for that, maybe we could, uhhh, well you know what I mean."

"Cuz, you are so crazy." Paula laughed. "But seriously, don't be so quick to dismiss him. You could be good for each other. I think you two can actually complement one another. You know you can help erase some of that steely edge off of him."

"And what can he do for me?"

"Well, he could help calm you down a little. You can get all hyped over nothing sometimes."

"Me?" Fantasia pointed at herself. "Please. I'm always cool as a cucumber."

"Yeah, right. Come on, let's hit Rodeo Drive. I'm ready to see some more of what this city has to offer."

"Sounds like a plan, because we're just getting this day started. There's still a lot to do, plenty more to see, more money to blow."

"All right. Let's do this."

Paula and Fantasia spent the remainder of the day, hanging out at some of LA's most famous boutiques. Fantasia loved to be in the lime light, and showing her best friend and cousin around the city was right up her alley. She wasn't conceited or vain, she simply loved the fact that she was in a position to go where she wanted to go, when she wanted to go and not worry about money or means. She was on top of the world, and she loved every minute of her success.

5

"When you trip over love, it is easy to get up. But when you fall in love, it is impossible to stand again." Albert Einstein

Sweet Taboo was getting closer to becoming a reality. The thought that she was finally going to open a gallery in Broknfield, gave Fantasia a huge boost of self-pride in her many accomplishments. She relaxed her head against the head cushion on her first class flight to Broknfield. She was anxious to see Paula and her kids. She couldn't believe that it had been two months since Paula's visit to Cali. She was also excited and anxious to see the space the developers had in mind for the gallery. Most of her meetings about Sweet Taboo had been conducted via Skype, online, and meetings in Cali with her capable staff.

Previously, she had spent two weeks in Belleaf following up on some international art deals she had going on there as well. Belleaf was the home office for her business. Just as she expected, everything was in tiptop shape when she arrived, and her mother was doing fine.

Fantasia's flight landed. She retrieved her luggage and proceeded out of the airport to wait on Paula. She went to Baggage Claim where Paula said she would be waiting. Ten minutes, fifteen minutes, thirty minutes passed and Fantasia was growing quite restless and slightly irritated after Paula still hadn't arrived. She retrieved her cell phone from her designer handbag and proceeded to call her cousin for the seventh time. Her call went straight to voice mail like the last six times. She had even texted Paula but didn't get a response.

Suddenly, a cinnabar red Mercedes SUV pulled up in front of her. Fantasia stepped back from the curb, unsure as to whether the fool behind the wheel was going to drive up on the curb and plow her down. *Probably on the daggone cell phone texting and not paying attention*, she thought.

The driver's door opened.

"Sorry I'm late. There was a backup on the interstate."

Fantasia's face turned redder than the color of the Mercedes. Her mouth was open but no words came out. Why was Randall here and not Paula?

"I know you were expecting your cousin, but she got a call from the school about one of the kids."

"Where is Nick?"

"In Seattle meeting with one of our distributors. So," he remarked with hands upraised, "that leaves me." He walked up to her and right away took hold of both pieces of her luggage. "How was your flight?" he asked like the two of them had been talking every day, when in reality she hadn't talked to Randall since he left California.

Fantasia didn't respond. She wished Paula had called or texted to explain what happened. She would have told Paula that she would take a taxi or call one of her business associates to pick her up.

"Aren't you going to at least say, hello?" Randall placed the luggage in the back of the Mercedes before walking to the passenger door and opening it for Fantasia.

"Uh, I...what did you say happened to Paula?"

"She's at the emergency room. Their youngest kid had an accident and broke her leg while she was on some kind of school outing. Paula said she's going to be okay, but I guess it goes without saying; she was not about to leave her kid's side."

"So, you still portraying to be Mr. Nice Guy, volunteered to come and pick me up, huh?" Fantasia spoke, a tinge of bitterness reflected in her voice.

"To be honest, I was hoping they could have found someone else. I'm a businessman, not an Uber driver. But then again, Nick is my business partner and Paula, well Paula being Paula, who can say no to her. She's such a sweet girl. So, here I am."

He stood patiently by the door until Fantasia, while rolling her eyes, reluctantly got into the SUV.

Randall closed the door, ran around to the driver's side, and got in just as the air traffic cop blew her whistle for automobiles to move on.

Neither one of them said anything to each other until Randall turned out of the terminal and on to a street packed with commuters.

"If I had known about the accident, I could have made other arrangements to get to my hotel." Fantasia snarled, refusing to look over at Randall. She had managed to sneak a peek at him when he got out of the SUV. He was dressed impeccably well in a tailored, modern, bronze three piece suit. Fantasia knew fashion. Right away she knew it had to be by Burberry and probably set Randall back at least a grand. He had good taste. She liked that.

"I don't mean to sound rushed, but I have an important business meeting in," he looked at his timepiece briefly, "in about an hour. So, where to, Ms. Lady?"

Fantasia pursed her lips. He was starting to really try her nerves. What happened to the supposedly perfect Randall from California? She should have known it was all a big front. His true colors were definitely showing on this otherwise gorgeous fall day. This Randall was arrogant and obnoxious, and she couldn't wait for him to get her to her destination.

"Hotel Monaco Portland."

"Ahh, the Hotel Monaco. Nothing but five-star for the lady. I'm not surprised." Randall chuckled lightly.

"And what do you mean by that?"

"By what?" Randall chuckled again while looking in his side mirror as he blended in with the traffic heading toward downtown Portland.

"Never mind." She folded her arms and looked out the window at the cars passing by. Like she used to do when she was a kid, she tried counting the different colors of cars that zoomed past, hoping it would take her mind off the arrogant, smart-mouthed man sitting next to her. She couldn't wait to get to the hotel so she wouldn't have to ever see him again. And she couldn't wait to talk to Paula. She was going to let her, and Nick, know that Randall was not the perfect guy he had them believing that he was.

"I thought you had such an important business meeting," Fantasia said as they stepped off the elevator.

She unlocked the door to her hotel suite before turning and telling Randall, Thank you for walking me to my room, even though I insisted that you didn't.

Randall shook his head, as he sat her luggage on the other side of the opened door without walking inside the room.

"You have a good one," he said, then turned away from her and walked away.

6

"Relationships sink when they have too many passengers." Unknown

"Fantasia, I know you've been in Broknfield for almost a week, and I hate we haven't been able to spend any real girl time together," Paula apologized. "But between Talisa breaking her leg and now Jenay with the flu, girl I'm about to pull my hair out by the roots."

"See, stuff like that is exactly why I can never see myself doing the wife and kids thing. Too much stress and drama. But anyway, I understand that being a mommy comes first for you, and my schedule has been jam packed practically since I landed. I've met with art dealers, the architect for the gallery, developers, and the list goes on."

"Well, hopefully you'll be able to put down your sketch pad long enough to at least come by for lunch. I can do that much; fix us a couple of sandwiches, a salad, and some chips. I can't let you come home to Broknfield and not spend any time with you."

"I'll try to stop by tomorrow afternoon. I still have some choice words for you for that stunt you pulled." Fantasia chuckled into the phone.

"What are you talking about?" Paula questioned.

"Girl, don't even go there. I told you that night when I got to the hotel that you knew what you were doing when you sent Randall to pick me up from the airport. You know you were trying to play Paula the matchmaker again."

"I told you then and I'm telling you now that was not my intention. You know I had a legitimate emergency, and there was no way I could come and get you. Randall was the only person I could find that was available. Hope and David are at one of their church conventions upstate so who else was I going to ask?"

"Whatever, Paula. You know if you had called me and told me the situation with Talisa that I would have called the hotel and had them send a driver or I could have called the hotel shuttle service, one of my business partners, Uber, somebody would have picked me up. Somebody other than him."

"Come on now, he's not that bad, is he?" asked Paula jokingly.

"I can't lie. He *is* fine, but you know how I am."

"What are you talking about? How are you?"

"I can't do the uptight, I go to church every Sunday, and say my prayers every night kind of guy."

Paula burst out laughing over the phone. "You are so crazy."

Fantasia laughed too. "I'm just telling you what y'all say God loves - the truth."

7

"Flirtationship: more than a friendship, less than a relationship." Unknown

"Hi, Fantasia, it's Randall. I was calling to check up on you. I know I'm probably the last guy you want to hear from, but I just finished up a meeting near your hotel. I'd like to know if you would care to join me for an early dinner."

Ummm, should I? Why should I? He's a jerk. "Then again, I don't have any more meetings or plans for the rest of the evening. I guess it can't hurt," she said as she laid down her briefcase on the hotel bed.

She had just finished another long day, finalizing the details for the gallery. Everything had gone rather smoothly and she was excited that another one of her dreams was about to come into full fruition. The only thing was that she didn't have anyone to celebrate her accomplishments with. She could call her mother and tell her the good news and Ruth would be overjoyed, but still somehow it just wouldn't be the same. Her brother, Prodigal, was consumed with his life and family, and rightfully so. Hope and her husband David were doing their own thing. Paula always congratulated her and told her how proud she was of her, but it wasn't the same.

Sometimes she thought about how different her life might be if she had that special man in it, like the one in her dreams. A man that would be proud of what she was achieving in her life.

She wanted someone to come home to, someone to hold her and make love to her. She had slept with a few men in her adult life and had regretted doing so every time. She had no problem dating, but she'd yet to meet *the one*. Her mother had been blessed to find another man who she loved deeply and who loved her. Now her mother was a happily married businesswoman with no worries whatsoever.

Fantasia contemplated Randall's invitation again as she tried to dismiss the bout of loneliness that had suddenly infiltrated her mind and spirit. She toyed with her phone then before she could change her mind, she hit the SEND button and returned Randall's call.

♥

Fantasia enjoyed a soothing bath, then got out of the tub and rushed to find something to wear. She didn't know why she suddenly felt a bout of nervousness. After all, it was just a friendly dinner with a man she didn't really care that much for. But she still found herself being extra careful to choose the perfect outfit.

It was raining, as usual, in Portland and as the sun set, the temperature dropped, so it was rather cool, almost on the verge of cold outside. She chose a stunning designer pants and shirt set and a pair of pumps.

After squirting on a hint of her favorite perfume, she checked to make sure her thick, deep burgundy dyed sisterlocks were perfectly held back off her face with a wide scarf that tied underneath the back of the long locks.

As she applied the finishing touches to her hair and stood in the full length mirror to give herself a once over, her text message notification sounded.

On my way up to get you. Is that all right?

"No need. I'm on my way down," she texted back.

She turned to go retrieve her clutch purse from the living room area. Without warning, she felt something weird. What was wrong with her? She tried to dismiss the feeling again, but there it was again – the pitter patter of her heart beat...followed by the flitter of butterflies in her belly.

8

"Judging someone is easy. Getting to know someone for who they really are takes effort."

Unknown

"Thanks for keeping me from dining alone," Randall told Fantasia as he sat across from her.

Fantasia barely wore makeup. She was more of a natural beauty. Her smooth skin, high cheekbones, and her smile, were perfect.

Fantasia looked at him and then quickly looked away. There it was again. That funny feeling in the pit of her stomach. She didn't like it. The last thing she needed to do was get sick. She had too much business to take care of, and she had to get it all done so she would be ready to fly to Belleaf in two days.

Fantasia remained silent, picking over her Caesar salad.

"Why are you so quiet?"

"I could say the same about you," Fantasia replied.

"So, tell me something."

Fantasia practically for the first time during their dinner stared Randall squarely in his eyes. "What do you want me to tell you?"

"Why don't you like me?"

Fantasia eased back, her eyes flittered for a second or two. She laid her fork down on her plate.

"What makes you think that I don't like you?"

"Come on, now. I know that I'm not exactly Prince Charming, but hey, I'm a nice guy. Really,

I am. Just give me a chance," he said with smiling, seductive eyes.

"If you're so nice, why do I have to give you a chance? Seems to me that I would have picked up on that automatically." She removed the napkin from her lap and dabbed her mouth with it.

"Maybe it's because you were too busy judging me, or should I say, too busy making sure that you didn't like me. You know, Fantasia, something tells me that you're a very bitter woman. And please don't take that in a bad way. I'm just saying that it seems like someone really did a number on your heart."

Randall took a bite of food, then leaned slightly back in his chair, taking in Fantasia's striking features. Why did she have to be so uptight?

Suddenly, and without warning, Fantasia wiped her mouth with the cloth napkin, placed it on the table, and abruptly stood up. "Thank you for dinner. But if you'll excuse me, I'm leaving. And don't bother getting up; I'll walk to the hotel. Oh, and this should be enough to cover my portion." She opened her purse, pulled out a $50 bill and laid it on the table. Her lips were tight and the irritation on her face was quite visible, matching the angry tone in her voice.

"Did I say something to offend you, again?" Randall asked, standing up also.

"You know what. I knew this was a bad idea, but I thought, hey, I'll give the guy a chance. After all, it's just dinner. But you managed to screw it up, once again, with your flawed perception of me."

Fantasia walked away from the table and toward the front door leading out of the restaurant. By the time he finished transacting the business of paying for their meal, Fantasia was nowhere to be seen. He ran out the door, looked up and down the street, but he didn't see her anywhere. He thought about going to her hotel to make sure she got back safely, but decided against it. From what he already surmised, Fantasia was a fiercely independent woman, and definitely stubborn. As for him, he called 'em like he saw it. Something or someone had hurt her, and made an otherwise beautiful woman into a bitter woman, but he didn't have time nor did he want to take the time to figure out what was really going on with her.

"I can't believe the nerve of that guy," Fantasia fumed as she stripped down to her underwear after having arrived back to her hotel room in record time. "He's nothing but a prick hiding behind his religion. I should have known better. Fantasia, you've got to be more careful about who you spend your time with, girl," she chastised herself as she came out the rest of her clothes. "Ugh, I'm so dang mad. If I never see him again, it will be too soon."

"What about lunch tomorrow. One work for you?," the text message from Paula read. "My house."

The text message broke her angry mood and she sat in the chair next to the hotel window and texted Paula back. "Sounds good. See you then. TTYL. Going to bed."

Fantasia almost popped up out of the chair when she heard the knock on her hotel door. She stood up, clad only in a bombshell pink Victoria's Secret panties and bra set.

"Yes, who is it?" she asked as she stood next to the chair.

"Randall."

"What do you want?" she asked as she approached the door. *What is he doing here?"*

"I wanted to make sure you made it to your hotel safely. And you dropped something out of your purse."

My purse? "What did I drop out of my purse?"

"Will you open the door? I promise I don't bite. I just want to return to you what you lost. Tell me, why did you leave like that?" he asked, talking from the other side.

"Because I had no idea I was dining with an insensitive, self-righteous prick," she exclaimed. "Now, if you don't mind, I need you to leave. You can take whatever you have of mine to the concierge and I'll get it from there."

"Look, please. Just let me apologize in person. At least you can do that much," he pleaded.

Fantasia had to admit that he did sound sincere. Fantasia didn't respond. Instead, she went to the hotel closet and retrieved her Louis Vuitton travel bag. Opening it, she pulled out a pair of neatly folded leggings and a matching top, slipped into both of them, and jetted back to the door.

As she opened the door wider, stepped aside and allowed him entrance, Randall first returned the fifty dollars, then he gave her her American Express card. She had no idea that it had fallen out of her purse. Next, he gave her a single red rose.

"What is this for?" she asked, studying the sweet smelling flower.

"A peace offering," he replied. "Look, I'm sorry that I offended you, Fantasia. I really didn't mean any harm. Trust me, I didn't."

Fantasia felt herself softening. "Look, thank you for returning my card." She hesitated before adding, "And the rose. And you didn't have to give my money back. I have no problem paying my way. Now, if you'll excuse me, I have a long day tomorrow. I need to get some rest."

Fantasia walked back to the door. That weird tingling in the pit of her belly returned when her eyes connected with Randall's. She could not help breathing in the intoxicating scent of his cologne as he moved inside her space. He stood so close she could feel the heat emanating from his body.

Randall couldn't ignore her beauty. He looked at her like he was photographing her with his eyes. His gaze unintentionally dropped from her eyes to her shoulders to her breasts. Without warning, he closed the door, stepped forward, and clasped her body tightly into his. "You're so beautiful," he whispered, his breath hot against her ear. He moved his mouth over hers, forcing her lips open with the thrust of his tongue.

His luscious lips caused shockwaves rippling through her. She dropped the credit card, the rose, and the fifty dollar bill to the floor. She was helpless as her body betrayed her, giving in to the hardness of his body as he sandwiched her against the wall. Her mind carried her to that sacred place that she dreamed of. She visualized the man in her dreams as Randall.

Suddenly she pushed him off of her. "You should leave. Now," she said, still trembling from the wave of desire she felt.

"I'm sorry. Sounds like I'm saying that a lot, huh."

"Just leave."

Raising his hands, he said, "Goodnight, Fantasia."

Randall walked out the door and down the long hallway.

Fantasia closed the door slowly. She leaned against it, her breath heavy, her heart racing, as she held her hand to her chest.

"Mercy." She sighed before she walked away from the door and back toward the bedroom.

9

*"It is difficult to know at what moment love begins;
it is less difficult to know that it has begun."*
                            Henry Wadsworth Longfellow

"Call me if you run into any snags when you get there," Nick told Randall as he drove up to the airport's Drop Off area. "I don't think you will, though. Those guys did a good job of addressing all of our concerns about the space. I don't see why we won't be able to move in and open up shop in the next six to eight weeks. What do you think?"

"I think everything is working out better than we could have expected. Of course, there's some work we need to do to meet the standards and specifications as our other NT stores. When I get to Cali and meet with them tomorrow, I'll be able to better gauge whether everything is set to move forward. We've gone over the contract with a fine tooth comb; everything looks good."

"Yeah, man, this is a huge blessing. I'm so ready to see the Rodeo Drive store open."

"Yeah, God is good, bro. Tomorrow's meeting will help finalize the plans. Once we get that inspection completed, and get the thumbs up, we can start getting things set to move in. I have several interviews lined up, too for some sales staff."

"Cool. We've already received a ton of resumes and applications online. If you need me give me a call. Otherwise, I'll head that way the middle of next week and we'll meet the contractors that are going to do the build out."

Nick pulled up to the drop off area, put the car in park, and he and Randall stepped out of the car, still talking.

"Hey, while you're there, why don't you give ol' girl a call?" Nick chuckled.

"No way. That's one chick that I plan to stay away from. I know she's Paula's cousin and all, but I told you, ole girl has issues. All I can do is pray for her." Randall laughed as they walked to the back of the car and retrieved his luggage.

"I hear you. Well, take care of business. We'll talk later this evening after your flight lands and you get settled. Your hotel room is reserved and your rental car is...well you know the drill."

"Yeah, I got it. Take it easy, bro. I'll see you next week," Randall told him. They gave each other dap. Randall grabbed the handles on one piece of his luggage, used the extended strap to put the other bag on his shoulder, and proceeded inside the airport terminal.

It had been three months since his encounter with Fantasia. He thought of the kiss, the way her body succumbed to his touch, but he'd not heard from the obviously mixed up woman since that night. There was a time or two, oh well, more than a time or two when Randall thought about her, but each time he pushed her out of his thoughts, other than to maybe say a quick prayer for her. He smiled at the thought of their last time together. He especially thought about how cute she looked even when she was mad. When Nick suggested that he call Fantasia since he would be in Cali for the next few months, opening the new store, Randall didn't know if that would be such a good idea. Fantasia probably wouldn't talk to him even if he did try calling her. She probably was no longer in Cali anyway. He remembered that her business was headquartered in Maryland; California was where she mostly came to get away from the rat race that was her life.

For the next several weeks, everything went as planned. He spent Christmas alone in his hotel room in California. To usher in the New Year, he attended a church he saw a commercial about on TV.

After the holidays, Nick flew down as planned. He and Randall met and discussed their plan for Randall to move to California so he could manage the store full time, while Nick managed the four other stores they owned in Oregon and Seattle. Randall would manage the other stores they planned on opening up in California over the next thirty-six months. He was grateful that he'd found a good business partner in Randall. He couldn't have asked for a better person to work with.

"Hey, did you talk to Fantasia over the holidays?" Randall asked Nick on one of his visits to Cali.

"Actually, we talked briefly a few days ago. She should still be in Belleaf. She said she would be flying back down here in a few days. She's thinking about relocating and opening a spot in San Francisco. Her mom is managing the one in Belleaf and she says it's pretty self-sufficient. She can fly there whenever she wants or needs to." Nick grinned.

"What's so funny?" Randall asked.

"Why are you asking about Fantasia? I thought you said she was a bitter woman with a serious mean streak that you had no time for."

"She is. I was asking out of curiosity, and for conversation. Even if I did decide to hit her up, it would only be to see how she's doing. You know what I mean?"

"Are you sure that's all?"

"What do you mean?"

'Man, come on. You're no school boy. You know what's up."

"Ha, no way." Randall chuckled.

10

"Sometimes it takes a painful experience to make us change our ways." Proverbs 20:30

Flying first class on a seven-hour flight from Maryland to California was exhausting, no matter how much the flight attendants catered to her needs. There was so much going on in her life. Not that she was complaining. She loved the life she lived, even during the times she seemed to be running around nonstop. The art world was hectic but still for her, it was rewarding. She had the opportunity and the means to jet all over the world and she couldn't see herself trading her lifestyle in for anything or anyone in the world. She often reflected on something the late Steve Jobs said, "Live each day like it's your last because one day it will be."

Her cell phone rang almost as soon as she stepped inside her Beverly Hills spread. She barely had time to plop down on the all-white sofa in her sprawling family room area.

Fantasia listened as the caller gave her the latest update about some business ideas Fantasia was toying with, then she shared her thoughts. "I understand, but after studying the plans and going over the demographics, I changed my mind. I think I'd like to open a gallery in NoHo or East Village. I'm not sure which one, maybe both. Heck, I may open three, one in NoHo, the East Village and Beverly Hills. I'll figure it out. What I am sure about is that I'm going to forego opening the store in Broknfield, at least for now. Of course, I still want to offer an after school and weekend art program where kids can come and learn about art at no cost," she explained to one of her assistants on the other end.

"Great decision," the man responded. "Do you want me to start scouting around for some suitable spaces in Broknfield and California for such a thing?"

"Yes, that will be super. You know my preferences." She chuckled lightly into the phone as she stood up and wandered around the open space.

"Yes, I do know you. Quite well, I'd like to think. I'll get started right away."

"Thanks. Oh, and if you will, please take care of my business calls for the remainder of the day. I just landed and I need some private time."

"I'm on it, Ms. Runsome."

Fantasia ended the call and was immediately greeted by Bianca. "Welcome back, Ms. Runsome."

"Hi, Bianca. Thank you. It is good to be back. Nothing can take the place of this," she said, looking around and walking toward the slide away doors leading out to the expansive backyard. "Who can pass up this million dollar view? It's addictive." Fantasia breathed in deeply, spread her arms out and looked out at the deep blue sky. "Will you make my usual?"

"Yes, ma'am. Are you going to be in here?"

"I'm going to go upstairs, take a shower, then go outside my bedroom and relax on the balcony. You can bring it up there in about twenty or thirty minutes."

"Yes, Ms. Runsome."

"Thank you, Bianca. It's so good to be back in Beverly Hills. This is beginning to feel more and more like home."

Bianca smiled. She had been working for Fantasia for the past five and a half years. Most of the time, her employer was in Maryland or out of the country; anywhere but in California. Even when she did come to California, Bianca had no complaints about Fantasia.

Fantasia compensated her staff rather well, and treated them with respect and dignity. Bianca actually felt like Fantasia was more of a friend rather than her employer. She had helped Bianca out financially a couple of years ago when her husband was laid off from his IT job. When he cheated on Bianca and left her for someone he met on his new job, a job that Fantasia had helped him get, it was Fantasia whose shoulder Bianca leaned on.

Bianca and her two kids moved into the guesthouse on Fantasia's property, and had been there ever since. As far as Bianca was concerned, she lived life like a princess, thanks to Fantasia Runsome. There was no way would she ever be disloyal to Fantasia. Whatever she could do to help her, Bianca promised herself, she would do it.

"What about something to eat?" Bianca asked.

"Uh, not right now. I ate that hideous airplane food, so I'm good for now. Maybe something later this evening, but make sure it's something light."

"Okay. I'll bring your drink up shortly."

"Thanks, Bianca." Fantasia turned around, but not before taking in another view of the city from her mountaintop mansion.

♥

As the piping warm streams of water massaged her body, without warning, Fantasia was betrayed by thoughts of Randall's kiss and his warm embrace. She shivered like she was cold. It was almost like he was standing next to her, holding her, caressing her, making love to her.

"No way," she said aloud. "The man who has my heart is only in my dreams. Only in my dreams," she repeated as she shook her head from side to side hoping to dispel the tempting thoughts.

11

"Someday someone might come into your life and love you the way you've always wanted." Unknown

"Fantasia, I need you," Nick said. "Please tell me you're still in California."

"Yes...I'm here. I told Paula I was going to be here indefinitely. What's wrong? You sound like your world has collapsed. Is Paula okay? What about the kids?"

"Yes, they're fine. It's Randall."

Fantasia's concern fizzled rather quickly when she realized that Nick was calling about Randall.

"Look, I don't want to hear about that man. When are you and Paula going to get it? I don't have time for that sanctimonious, obnoxious..."

"Randall is in the hospital. He's in critical condition."

"What? What happened?"

"He was robbed and carjacked."

"Robbed? Carjacked? When? Where? And what does all this have to do with me?"

Fantasia hated to hear this news, but she was still somewhat confused. Why did Nick feel that he needed to tell her? She hadn't seen or heard from Randall since the last time she was in Oregon, and that had been months ago.

"I don't get it. I mean, I'm sorry to hear this, but I still don't understand."

"He's there."

"There? Here? Are you saying he's in California?"

"Yes!" Nick all but yelled in the phone. He realized he must have sounded like a rambling idiot of some kind. He hadn't taken the time to explain to Fantasia that Randall had been assaulted in California the night before.

"Look, I'm sorry, Fantasia. I guess I'm not making myself clear."

"No you're not. But calm down. Tell me what's going on."

"From what I've learned, Randall was leaving from one of our distributor's place of business last night. Two guys ambushed him when he stopped at the gas station. From what the cops tell me, they must have watched him pump his gas, and before he could pull off the gas station lot, one of them pulled a gun on him, jumped in the car followed by another guy. They had him drive to the rear of the gas station. They robbed him and beat him up pretty bad, left him lying there unconscious. Probably for dead."

"Oh no, that's horrible." Fantasia's left hand went over her heart. "Is he going to be okay?"

"Like I said, he's in bad shape. All they would tell me is that he sustained a head injury. I'm just grateful that they found my business card on him and called me. Otherwise, there's no telling when I would have found out he'd been carjacked."

"This is terrible. I really hate this for him." Fantasia felt tears forming but she refused to let them fall. She could count the times she'd shed a tear since her father died over twenty years ago, so she wasn't about to cry over someone she barely knew. What she couldn't understand was why in the world she felt like crying anyway. She shook her head, sort of bucked her eyes, and tried to shake off the feeling of sadness and heartache that was trying to come over her. Randall was a nice man, and though she would never admit it to anyone, he may even be a great guy, but he wasn't worth shedding her tears over. No man was. Not in her book.

"Look, I'm trying to get a flight as soon as I can, but I'm still out of the country."

"Out of the country? Where are you?"

"Dubai, at Arab Fashion Week. I'm here checking out some of the latest men fashions to hopefully add to our Beverly Hills spot."

"Oh, okay."

"Is there any way you can go to the hospital?"

"What about his family? Have you contacted his parents?"

"Randall doesn't have any family."

"He has no family? No siblings? A girlfriend? Surely he has someone."

Fantasia hadn't bothered to ask anything before now about Randall's background as far as family was concerned. She was shocked when Nick told her that both of Randall's parents and his younger sister died during Hurricane Katrina. From what Nick told her, Randall was away at college at the time and his parents and sister had gone to New Orleans for a church convention.

"I didn't know that he had no family. I'm so sorry. What hospital is he in?" Fantasia asked.

"Cedars-Sinai. Look, I promise I'll be there as soon as I can, hopefully in a few days."

"Let me write down his information. I want to be sure they'll let me see him since he has no next of kin."

"If you have any problem, just call me or have them call me or tell them you're his wife. Whatever you have to do, do it. I just need him to know that he has someone there for him."

"Okay. I'm on the way there."

"Thank you, Fantasia."

Fantasia hurriedly ended the call, told Bianca where she was headed, and then took off to the hospital.

On her drive to the hospital, Fantasia hoped that Randall would pull through. Nick had said he was in critical condition, so she wasn't sure what to expect when she arrived. She had her issues with him, but never in life would she have wished something like this on him.

12

*"It doesn't matter who hurt you or broke you
down; what matters is who made you smile again."*
Kushandwizoom

Watching a heavily sedated Randall lying in a
hospital bed connected to tubes, tore at
Fantasia's heart. She fought back tears again as
she studied his bruised and swollen face. He
was barely recognizable. Carefully, she took hold
of one of his hands and gently caressed it back
and forth.

"Randall, you're not alone. It's me, Fantasia,"
she whispered. "I'm here with you. I'm not going
to leave you." She used her free hand to wipe
away the tears that finally burst forth and
streamed down her face. Painful memories of her
father's death flooded her mind. She was just a
little girl when he died, but she still vividly
remembered him and missed him terribly. She
thought about when her only brother, Prodigal,
was burned and lost his leg from a fire he was
fighting in Oregon some years ago. She thought
about Prodigal's late wife, Faith, and her long,
painful battle with cancer. Cancer won. Life was
so unfair, but more than that, she felt like God
was unfair. Fantasia felt a sense of dread come
over her. Grief surrounded her heart to the point
that she felt like she was about to suffocate.
Now, seeing Randall like this, was almost too
much for her to bear, but she had to be strong
for him, especially since Nick said he didn't have
any family.

Fantasia released his hand momentarily to focus her attention on pulling up a chair to sit next to his bed. She sat down in the chair and took hold of his hand again.

"Are you his wife?" a nurse asked, startling Fantasia when she walked into Randall's room.

"Uh, no.... I'm his sister," she said before she realized how easily the lie flowed from her lips. "How is he? Is he going to be okay?"

"He took a pretty severe beating, but from what the doctor says, he should pull through. It may take some time, and there's swelling on his brain, which is why he's sedated right now. The doctor wants to give his brain time to heal and for the swelling to go down."

"When will the doctor be here?"

"He will be making his rounds later this afternoon."

"Okay, thank you," Fantasia replied, watching the nurse check Randall's vitals.

"Is there anything you need?" the nurse asked Fantasia before she exited the room.

"No, but thank you for asking."

"Well, if you need anything, just push the button or come to the nurses' station."

"Thank you so much," Fantasia said.

The nurse left the room and Fantasia focused her attention back on Randall. She watched him for several more minutes before she called Nick. When he answered the phone, she told him what the nurse said and let him know that she would be by his bedside as long as she possibly could.

Nick immediately felt better knowing that Randall wouldn't have to go through this ordeal alone. Whether Fantasia recognized it or not, Nick's prayers had been answered. He had been praying since he was notified of Randall's injuries. He prayed for God not to let Randall be alone. He didn't know how long it would be before he was able to leave Dubai, but knowing Fantasia was with Randall gave Nick some much needed relief. No matter how much or matter of fact Fantasia wanted others to think she was, Nick knew that she could be compassionate and possessed a heart of gold.

He breathed a sigh of relief as he listened to Fantasia talk about Randall and what a great person he was. He managed to smile over the phone as he heard the genuine concern in her voice. Maybe she didn't realize it, but Nick sure did. Fantasia sounded like a woman in love.

"I'm going to spend the night," she explained to Nick. "When I hang up from talking to you, I'm going to call Bianca and ask her if she will bring me some toiletry items and a change of clothes. I can take a shower here. That way I'll be here whenever the doctor comes in, and when Randall wakes up, he'll see that he isn't alone. Although I don't know how he'll react when he opens his eyes and sees my face," Fantasia said with a slight grin on her lips.

"I'm sure you'll be a sight for sore eyes," Nick said and chuckled.

"Yeah, right," Fantasia responded. "I can't believe someone would do him like this, Nick. He looks awful. He's battered and bruised, his eyes are swollen shut and he looks like, well like a monster." She started crying again.

"Hey, calm down. Everything is going to be all right. Randall is a fighter and a man of faith. God isn't through with him yet."

"Please don't start your God talk. If God was so great and all, then Randall wouldn't be lying in this bed and none of this would have happened. So, I don't want to hear it. This only confirms my beliefs. When Randall wakes up, maybe he'll finally see that he can't depend on God to protect him. He should have been strapped with a gun and then those thugs would be laying here instead of him."

"You're so daggone stubborn, Fantasia. But, hey, I'm not madatcha. I'm thankful that Randall has you there. Look, I've gotta go. I have another meeting in a few. I'll call you later and check on my buddy."

"Okay, talk to you later. Bye, Nick."

Bye, and thanks again. I know Randall is going to be grateful for what you're doing."

"I'm doing it for you, not Randall," she stated hoping she could convince herself that she meant what she said.

13

"I'm addicted to the way I feel when I'm thinking about you." Unknown

Randall's recovery improved drastically over the next ten days. The brain swelling had gone down, he was no longer being heavily sedated, and the only evidence that he'd been assaulted were a few gashes and cuts remaining on his face. The brain injury that the neurologist believed would be traumatic turned out to be not as serious as predicted. Doctors told him that it was nothing short of a miracle.

He still had a ways to go before he would fully recover and return to his normal routine, but Randall was extremely grateful and gave praises to God every time he thought about what could have happened.

"I can't thank you enough for letting me stay here," Randall told Fantasia as he sat around the pool area at her house. As he spoke, his words were still a little slow. Sometimes Fantasia detected a slight slur in his voice, but the neurologist said that was to be expected. The blows he took to the head would take time to heal. One of the side effects was his speech and he still had difficulty walking.

"Well, contrary to what you might think, I can be a sympathetic soul."

"I never thought anything otherwise. You're the one that walks around trying to wear that hard shell. But I believe I have great spiritual discernment, and I felt your kind spirit from the first moment I met you. I think it's what drew me to you."

"Drew you to me?" Fantasia looked baffled. She felt her stomach growing all tingly and nervous inside. Why did he have that effect on her? What was it about Randall Hughes that caused her heart to flutter and her tummy to bubble? Her mind flashed back again to the time they were in Oregon. His touch, his kiss and his embrace replayed in her mind. She watched him intensely as he sat across from her. Speechless, she tried to remove the intimate thoughts of him from her mind.

Sounds of distress brought her back to reality, and she quickly pounced up from her chair when she saw the look of pain spread across his handsome face.

"What's wrong?" She said, hurrying over to his side.

"Ughhh," he moaned as his face twisted and contorted. "Another one...." He tried to move but almost fell out of the chair, screaming in agony.

Fantasia grabbed hold of his arm and the chair while screaming for Pedro, Bianca's brother and one of her personal chefs, to come to their aide. Within less than a minute, Pedro was at Randall's side. He helped him stand, and then at Fantasia's prompting, assisted Randall in going inside the house. He was still not fully capable of maintaining his full balance, so Pedro gave him the cane Randall used.

"Take your time. Pedro, please help him to his room."

"I'm not an invalid," Randall snapped. "And I'm not a child."

"I was only trying to help," she replied. "Don't get mad at me. And as for being a child, well you sure are whining like one, like a lil' girl to be exact."

Randall gave her a scowling look. "Thank you, Pedro I can make it from here."

Pedro looked over at Fantasia who was standing on the other side of Randall, like he was seeking her approval first.

Fantasia nodded and Pedro walked away slowly, but not before stopping, looking back over his shoulder and making sure Randall was stable enough to go to one of the downstairs bedrooms that Fantasia had set up solely for his use.

Randall often experienced excruciating spasms three or more times a day. He described them as starting in his neck and moving halfway up his head. He said it felt like his brain was moving or something. It lasted a few seconds at a time, but it was painful enough that it caused him major discomfort. The doctor explained that he might experience them for quite some time.

"Is there anything I can get you?" Fantasia asked once Randall sat down on the bed.

With careful precision, Randall eased back against the fluffy, plush pillow, exhaling slowly. "I'm good."

"Are you sure? If you like, I can get you one of your muscle relaxers, something to eat, anything, just name it."

"I said, no! Stop treating me like I'm some helpless old man. I had a minor spasm and you're treating me like I'm your kid or something. Leave me alone!"

Randall really did appreciate Fantasia for taking him in while he was recuperating. He was in a rehabilitation facility for a week after being discharged from the hospital. He could have flown back to his apartment in Oregon, but doctors advised against it, so Fantasia insisted that he recuperate at her house.

Randall basically had no choice. But he told himself that it would only be for a few weeks and then he would be strong enough to continue his search for a place of his own in Cali, something he had been doing before his attack.

"Fine," she screamed back. "Have it your way. I'm only trying to be nice to you."

"Nice to me? Look, lady. I don't need or want your pity!"

"Is that what you think this is? Pity? For your information, I don't feel pity for you. As a matter of fact, I don't feel a darn thing for you! If it wasn't for Paula and Nick, you wouldn't be here anyway! So how's that for *pity*," she shouted, walking swiftly out of Randall's room before he could say another word. Fantasia stormed out of his room, slamming his bedroom door behind her.

"He is going through a lot, Ms. Runsome," Bianca said, meeting her in the hallway. The two of them were mere inches from colliding into one another.

"I don't know what to do, Bianca. All I'm trying to do is help him until he is strong enough to get back up and on his own." Fantasia was just about in tears. How dare Randall shoot off on her like she was nobody when she was the one who had opened her home up to him. This was a perfect example of hypocrisy in her book. Here Randall was always telling her stuff about God but look how he was treating her.

"Bianca, it's not my fault that this happened to him."

"He knows that, senorita. But give him a break. He is still in pain. Both physically and emotionally. He is not fully well. It must be hard for him to have to rely on your kindness. Men can be that way."

Fantasia folded her arms. Walking beside Bianca along the hallway, she thought about what Bianca said. "But didn't you hear how he was yelling?"

"Like I say to you, he's not himself. He was badly injured. Time will heal his body - and his heart. You'll see. But you must be patient."

"I'm sorry, but patience is not one of my strong suits, especially with someone like Randall Hughes."

14

"You're my dream; please come true." Unknown

For the next several days Fantasia didn't go and check in on Randall like she had previously done since he unofficially moved in her home. Instead, she asked Bianca and Pedro to attend to his needs. From their report, he was improving considerably.

Before retiring for the evening, Fantasia drifted down the hallway toward Randall's room. His door was slightly ajar. Fantasia peeped inside. No Randall. She stuck her head in a little farther and scoped the large bedroom. No Randall. She figured he was probably in the bathroom and started walking off, but stopped when she heard the baritone voice behind her.

"Looking for me?" Randall asked.

Fantasia grabbed her chest and turned around. "Ugh, no. I see that you're walking without your cane. You must be feeling better," she said dryly.

"As a matter of fact, I am. I think in the next week or two I'll be ready to make a move."

"I don't think you have to be concerned with that," the female voice said as she appeared in the doorway of Randall's room.

The unfamiliar voice startled Fantasia. She looked pass Randall and saw a pencil thin, petite brunette.

"Who are you?" Fantasia asked.

The female stranger interloped her arm through Randall's arm."

"Oh, I'm sorry. I didn't mean to be impolite, not after everything you're doing for Randy." The woman extended her free hand out toward Fantasia. "I'm Hilary, Randy's fiancé."

Fantasia ignored the woman's hand and instead gave Randall a look that could kill. Fantasia couldn't believe what she was hearing. No this fool didn't have some strange woman up in her house saying she was his fiancé. He had his nerve.

Randall gave the woman a confused look. "*Ex*," he said with emphasis.

"I see. So where have you been all this time? I mean, being that you are *Randy's* fiancé."

"Actually, I just flew in from Memphis. That's where I lived and worked until a few weeks ago. Anyway, I'm here now. I'm going to take care of you, baby."

"Ohhh, that's nice," Fantasia said. "I wish I had known you were coming, I would have made preparations."

"Thank you," Hilary said, clinging to Randall.

"Look, Hilary, just chill, will ya. Go in my room. I need to talk to Fantasia for a minute."

"Nice meeting you, Fantasia," Hilary said, smiling.

"And you as well." Fantasia feigned.

Hilary folded her hands and walked into Randall's bedroom.

"Fantasia, I didn't know she was coming here," he explained.

"She's your fiancé, why wouldn't she come and see about you."

Why hadn't Nick told her that Randall was engaged, and why was she so angry. Was it because Hilary was an uninvited guest in her home or was it because the woman was Randall's fiancé? No that couldn't be it. Fantasia was not jealous of any female so there was no way she could be experiencing the green-eyed monster, could she.

"What I'm saying is that I didn't know she was coming until she was here in Cali. And she is no longer my fiancé," he said as he guided her up the hall. "We were engaged, but that's been over and done with for over a year."

Randall didn't want a wedge between him and Fantasia. She had been good to him; opening her home and her heart to him the way that she had. As for Hilary, he had finally given in to her incessant calls. It was during one of those days when he was feeling bad, thinking about the attack, his condition, and feeling helpless and forlorn all at the same time. It was late at night when she called and so he answered and found himself telling her everything that had happened the past weeks pertaining to his assault. He told her about Fantasia allowing him to recuperate at her spread. When she had told him she had left the company where she worked in Memphis for a once in a lifetime job offer in Phoenix, he was genuinely happy for her. A few days after they talked, she called and said she was in California on business, and wanted to know if it would be all right if she came by to see how he was doing.

He didn't see a problem with it, especially since he explained to Hilary his living situation, but typical Hilary acted oblivious to the fact that things were over between them. She came prancing into Fantasia's spread acting like she was still his woman. As much as he appreciated her, anyone for that matter, being concerned about his well-being, he didn't want Hilary to get any ideas. He would never take her back.

"Just give me a minute. Hilary will be leaving soon. She's in Cali on business, so she won't be here long. She wanted to come by to see how I was doing."

"I understand. Really I do. It's just that I'm not used to people dropping in on me. It's one of the reasons I had this house built in the mountains in this secluded gated community."

"I know, and again I'm sorry. Look, I guess it's no better time to tell you than now."

"Tell me what?" Fantasia said bitterly.

"I've taken up enough of your time and your space. I appreciate everything you've done to help me, but I think it's time for me to make a move."

"Make a move where? From what Nick said, you hadn't had a chance to do any real house hunting before the carjacking."

"It shouldn't be that difficult to find a spot here. It doesn't take much for me anyway. A one bedroom place will be cool. Since I'm feeling better, I've been looking a little online. But, hey, that's not your worry. You've done enough good deeds for me. I owe you."

Randall was just inches from her. His tall stature compared to her demure one made her feel vulnerable and a little nervous.

"You don't owe me a thing. But, hey, suit yourself. If you need some help in finding a place, let me know. I can have my realtor to do some research. Oh, what am I saying? You have Hilary for that. I'm sure she'll be more than happy to help you find a spot."

"You know what?"

"What?" Fantasia walked into the family room, and stopped.

"You may not see it, but I do."

"See what?" she asked.

"Your spirit."

Fantasia laughed.

"And an even more beautiful laugh," he said as he stepped closer to her.

Fantasia quickly stepped away.

"I'm not going to bite. You should know me better than that by now." He smiled and his pearly whites drew her into him like a moth to a flame.

He leaned in and kissed her on the cheek. "Thank you for everything."

"Sure, *Raaandy*," Fantasia said with a bite of sarcasm as she turned and walked off hurriedly. She didn't trust what she was feeling on the inside. It had been some time since she had succumbed to her fleshly desires and given her goodies up. She tended to think that sex was overrated anyway and could staunch one's success in life. So many women today got all wrapped up and went head over heels for a man, only to have him break her heart and ruin her life. Fantasia was determined not to be one of those stupid, weak types of women. And she wasn't like some of her female art clients and even friends that she and Paula knew nothing more than THOTs. There was one perfect man for Fantasia, and that man was only in her dreams.

15

"I knew the first time we met you'd kinda be hard to forget." Unknown

Hilary remained in California for a week. She came to see Randall every day. Fantasia and Hilary talked and Hilary told her all the wonderful and exciting things about her and Randy's relationship. She confessed that they had their share of problems, but she never gave Fantasia any indication that Randy and her had parted ways.

Hilary regretted cheating on Randall. She had messed up a good thing, and for that she was sorry. Randy, which she called him almost from the first time they met, was a good guy. She had prayed that he would forgive her infidelity, and although he said that he had forgiven her long ago, he still would not entertain them getting back together.

On her last day before she got ready to return to Phoenix, she and Randall went out to lunch. Her hopes were further dashed when Randall thanked her for coming but reemphasized that their relationship was done and that there would be no turning back.

Hilary left California with a heavy heart, but Randall felt that finally she understood that they could only be friends.

Later that evening, while sitting outside enjoying the sunset, Randall thought about his life and everything that had transpired over the years, such as the death of his parents and sister. He thought about the ending of the relationship between him and Hilary, the girl he believed at one time was his forever love. About how hurt he felt when he discovered that she had been unfaithful. The more he thought about his life, the more he seemed to fall into a funk. He felt alone even though he knew that God was on his side. The imperfect human part of him felt troubled and sad. When he replayed the assault and carjacking over in his mind, and the fact that he was still crippled from it, he hit his fist on the table next to the lounge chair that he was seated in.

"What do you want from me?" he screamed as he looked out over the horizon.

He didn't hear nor see Fantasia as she came out to the patio and stood behind him. She listened to his prayers without saying a word. With a bowed down head and sympathetic heart, she quietly strolled over to where he sat with his head now buried in his hands.

She kneeled down beside him. Somewhat startled, Randall popped his head up and looked over at her. His bloodshot eyes revealed the depth of his pain.

Fantasia stroked his back. "It's going to be all right. I know it is," she said softly.

She continued to caress him and talk to him. She hated to see him or anyone for that matter in pain. Pain was something she understood, something she had lived through. The thought that Randall was experiencing it was almost more than she could bear.

"Why don't you go inside and get some rest. You've had a long day."

Randall managed a smile. "I told you that you were sweet."

Fantasia smiled back. "When I want to be. I don't mean to pry, but did Hilary leave? I know you said her flight was supposed to depart earlier today."

"Yeah, she's gone. I think I finally got through to her that we're done. Did I love her once? Yeah, I did. But it didn't work out for us. And to be honest, I'm glad I found out before we exchanged vows. You know what I mean?"

"I think I do," Fantasia said. "I've never been engaged or in love," she confessed, "but I know how it feels to be hurt and heartbroken, and I don't wish it on my worst enemy."

"Thanks for understanding. And just know that I didn't mean to show any disregard for this being your home and for you allowing me to stay here. But Hilary can be stubborn and demanding."

"She was no problem. For real. Maybe you needed to see her so you two could resolve your past issues. Now that you have, maybe she can move on with her life."

"Yeah, maybe both of us can. Thanks, Fantasia."

"For what?"

"For listening without judging."

"No problem."

Randall caressed the side of her face. Slowly and gently he moved his hand from the side of her cheek and around her neck, and leaned in to kiss her. With ease, he guided her on to his body. Without protest Fantasia gave in to her desires. What could it hurt anyway? She was a grown woman and this grown woman wanted to feel exactly the way she was feeling now – loved.

This time there was no stopping, no holding back. A little awkward at first, they both managed to remove the barriers of clothing that stood between them fully unleashing their desires.

As she closed her eyes, and gave Randall access to her totally, her mind, her body, and her heart experienced all the magical feelings she dreamed about. It was good. Just like the man in her dreams.

Fantasia's eyes opened. She looked from the right and then to the left. She lay in her bed; her empty bed. It took her a moment or two to realize that she had been dreaming. She thought about the dream and the fact that Randall was making love to her. She shook her head like she was trying to shake away what she was feeling on the inside.

Sitting up in her bed, she then got up, grabbed her robe from off the nearby chair and walked downstairs to make herself some chamomile tea.

16

"A simple hello could lead to a million things."
Unknown

Randall searched online for an apartment now that he was getting around better and feeling almost back to his normal self. He was even transacting company business online via Skype or on his phone. Weeks had passed since the carjacking. The police had finally caught the thugs responsible for the crazy situation that was his life.

Nick would be flying in the following day. The two of them were going to get out and take a look at some of the apartments and lofts he found. It was time for him to give Fantasia her life back. He would be lying if he said that he didn't enjoy being around her, but no man wanted to feel helpless and at the mercy of a woman. At least not Randall. He wanted to be the one to invite Fantasia or any woman he chose over to his own place and have her in his own space. Now that he was feeling close to one hundred again, he couldn't wait to hang out and really enjoy life again.

Randall was attracted to Fantasia but on the other end, he wasn't one to chase after a woman. His career took precedence in his life and he wasn't one to hop in the bed with just any female. He'd had more than his share of companions, but there had been only one woman that he was serious about, and that had been Hilary.

Randall and Hilary met when one of his frat brothers asked him to take her out so he could take her best friend out. They hit it off and had been a couple up until she cheated.

When he was in college, he felt free to do and be what he wanted. Being raised in a strict Christian family, he couldn't freely date or hangout with friends. College was totally different. He was popular and women told him all the time how handsome he was, so he definitely did his share of making the girls happy. But he wasn't a young college dude anymore. He was a grown man, an entrepreneur trying to make his mark in the world. He wanted to enjoy financial wealth and success so he could help others and live the life he'd always dreamed of. No more wildin' out for him.

He shut down his Mac and turned on the television. He was going to watch a game and afterwards go to the fitness room and work out a little. Now that he was sturdier on his feet, he understood the only way for him to make a full recovery was to push his body. That meant he had to resume exercising.

After working out he swam several laps. The water felt good. He was thankful that God had spared his life. Those two guys could easily have killed him. He climbed out of the pool and went and laid out on the chaise. The moon was bright and made for a euphoric glow against the dark star-studded sky line. He looked to his right and studied the outline of the mountains. He turned to his left. He saw her silhouette.

"What are you doing out here by yourself? You haven't fully regained your strength. You still need to be careful."

"Are you sure you don't have kids somewhere?" Randall asked, then smiled.

"You know what, you can be a real butt hole at times."

"Me? How am I being a butt hole? I'm just saying. I mean you have such a maternal instinct. It's crazy."

"Yeah right, Randall. Make your jokes."

She was close enough for Randall to reach out and pull her to him, and that's exactly what he did.

Fantasia relived last night's dream as he took hold of her hand and gently tugged at her. Not hard, but enough that she was forced to come closer. She did, much to Randall's surprise, she didn't pull away. He pulled her down on his lap and even if she wanted to protest, his lips covered hers while his hands familiarized themselves with her body.

Fantasia melted like butter in his arms. The thin soft jumper she wore made it easy for him to explore. She kissed him back, while wrapping her hands around his shoulders and back. Her heart raced. Her body shuttered. She told herself to enjoy the moment; don't fight against it. She told her mind and heart that Randall was convenient and safe and that he would be gone in the next week or so. She even had plans to return to Belleaf in the next few weeks. It was time to check on the home office and her mom.

She pulled away from Randall, but just long enough to stand up, take hold of his hand so she could lead him to her room or his. There was no time for behaving like a little high school girl when she was quite the opposite. She was a woman who knew what she wanted, when she wanted it and she was used to getting whatever or *who*ever she wanted.

What she didn't know—so was Randall.

♥

Fantasia sat pretzel style on her bed. "Olivia, schedule me a flight leaving anytime tomorrow afternoon. I'm going home. I'm going to Belleaf," she told her personal assistant then ended the call.

Randall strolled out of the shower, reached for the white cotton towel hanging on the towel warmer and walked into his bedroom.

Ring. Ring.

His cell phone rang but the caller had hung up by the time Randall found it inside his slacks. Looking at his phone it started ringing again.

"Hello."

He listened as the realtor apologized for calling late, but he told him about a brand new listing for a townhouse. It would be the perfect place for Randall the realtor told him. He wanted to meet him first thing the following morning and if Randall liked it, he could put in his offer.

Randall agreed, hung up the phone and stretched back on the bed.

He thought of Fantasia and how she was used to having things her way. As badly as he wanted her, he had turned down making love to her. He desperately wanted her, but he wanted to practice self-restraint too. He didn't want a one night stand; he'd had more than his share of those. He prayed every night for God to show him the woman he was to spend the rest of his life with. There were moments when he had entertained that woman being Fantasia. That always made him laugh.

17

"Find someone that knows that you're not perfect but treats you as if you are." Unknown

"Please make up your mind what you're going to do," Paula told Fantasia as they Facetimed. "I mean, all this flying back and forth from Maryland to California, California to Maryland, is too much."

"I have a business here in Belleaf, Paula, or did you somehow forget that?"

"No, I haven't but you're the one who said that Aunt Ruth was the woman in charge. You said she could operate it better than you."

"She can and she does, but she's not the CEO, I am. She's not an artist and there are times my clients, new and old, want to see me. They want to talk to me and not just over Skype or Facetime. Plus, no matter where my home base is, my career means traveling. I travel all over the world, Paula. I'm not one to settle down in one place, you know."

"Whatever. Have you talked to Randall since you ran off a couple of weeks ago?"

"For your information, I did not run-off. And no, I haven't talked to him, nor do I want to talk to him."

"Okay, so he turned down your offer to get him between the sheets. I think it was admirable of him. Shows that he's not just out to screw you and move on."

"That's the problem I have with him. He's too serious. What guy in his right mind turns down the offer to sleep with a woman? Who does that?"

"Well, I think he likes you and I think you like him too. I just wish you two would stop all of the games and admit that you have the hots for each other."

"Maybe he and Hilary hooked back up. I wouldn't be surprised if they did."

"From what you said, she's not who he wants to be with. If he did, when she flew to California to see him, they would have worked things out. But what does he do? He practically sends her packing," said Paula.

"Let's change the subject please. I don't want to talk about Mr. Perfect, or *Randy* as Hilary calls him. Their relationship is none of my business anyway."

"Whatever. When are you coming back this way?"

"I don't know. I'll let you know. How are my little munchkin cousins?"

"They're good. Nick and I have been talking about taking them to Disneyland during their fall break."

"They'll like that. I might try to fly down around that time so I can see them."

"Cool," Paula squealed. "Hey, I have an idea."

"Uh uh, I don't like the sound of this." Fantasia made an ugly face. Paula laughed.

"No, listen. You should come with us. The kids would love it. I'm sure Nick would love it too because that would give him an excuse not to go all over California shopping and spending money with me and the kids. He and Randall can do their guy stuff, transact company business, watch football, or whatever. Please, say you'll come, Tasia."

"There you go, calling me, Tasia. The only time you do that is when you want me to feel guilty and give in to your demands."

Paula made a pouty face and said, "Well, did it work?"

"Ohh, okay. I'll think about it. Send me the details and I'll see you in a few weeks. Now look, I have to get back to work. Mom isn't feeling the best and I have a hundred and one things to do. It feels like ages since I've been in this office."

"Okay, love you!" Paula said, blowing a kiss into the phone. "Tell Aunt Ruth that I hope she feels better."

"Okay, I'll tell her. Love you. Talk to you later."

They signed off their Facetime session and Fantasia relaxed back in her chair.

Ruth knocked on the door and walked inside Fantasia's office.

"Hi, sweetie."

"Hi, Mama. Come on in."

Ruth walked up to her daughter's desk, sat in the chair in front of it, then clasped her hands.

"How are you, Ma? You look a little flushed."

"Just a little nauseated and short of breath. I think I have a stomach virus. Other than that, I'm blessed, honey."

"You taking something?"

"No, it's nothing that's keeping me down. But I wanted to let you know that I'm going to go home and get some rest."

"You can always go upstairs to the apartment and rest you know."

"No, I'm going to answer a couple of emails then I'm leaving."

"Okay, suit yourself. How is Moses? You haven't passed the bug on to him have you?"

"No. He's good."

"I'm glad to hear that. I haven't seen him since I got back. The three of us should have dinner when you feel better."

"That sounds good. Did you meet anyone while you were in California? I noticed that you stayed there longer than you typically stay."

"Mama, you know me. I'm not looking for anyone."

"I'm still praying about that. I'm telling you, I feel like God is orchestrating everything to work out for you. Your Moses is on the way. I'm telling you."

"That's wishful thinking on your end, but I'm not going to fuss with you. You and I both know that Moses is not like the typical male."

Ruth blushed. "You're right about that. I tell anyone who'll listen that Moses is a godsend. Never in a million years did I think I could be happy again, not after Solumun died. But God."

"I'm happy that you're happy. I agree with you; Moses is a good man. And he loves you."

"I'm going to keep the faith for that special someone to come into your life, Fantasia."

"Don't waste your prayers on me, Mama. Me and love will never be on one accord." Fantasia smirked, moving a few papers around on her desk.

"You sure you haven't met anyone?" Ruth asked.

"No. Not really."

"What do you mean *not really*? Sounds like you have met someone. Tell me about him."

"There's nothing to tell. Well, it's this guy I met. Mama, he is so arrogant. He thinks he knows it all, and I can't stand him. Oh, oh, and he's like you and Ruth, you know all into his faith. Ugh. Do you know that he even turned me down."

"Turned you down? How?"

"I know this may be too much information for you, but I'm going to tell you anyway."

"There's nothing this senior citizen hasn't heard. So let me hear it." Ruth laughed.

"He refused to sleep with me."

"Honey, that's admirable on his part. He probably respects you too much to have casual sex. Wait a minute, isn't this the young man that you let stay at your house because he was in some sort of accident?"

"Yeah, he's one in the same. Nick's business partner."

"Is he well?"

"Oh, yes. He's been up and around for a minute. Mama, he's just so.... he's too self-righteous and he's just, I don't know how to put it. It could never work with him. He was engaged but they broke up a while back."

"What does that have to do with anything? He isn't engaged now, right?"

"Right."

"Then something must have happened that made him or the both of them realize that it wasn't meant for them. As for you, I'm sure he sees the same beautiful, smart, intelligent young woman that I see."

"Sure, Mama. Anyway, I haven't talked to him anymore and I don't want to talk to him." Fantasia pretended to do some busy work, looking away from her mom and focusing on her computer screen.

"Um hmm," Ruth smiled. "What's his name?"

"Randall."

"Well, it sounds like you like Randall."

"Did you hear anything I just said? We don't get along. We're always at each other's throats." Fantasia shook her head. "He's so cocky."

Ruth chuckled some more. "Maybe he's just confident in who he is. As for his beliefs, how many times have I told you how important it is to have a relationship with God. I'm not talking about going to church every Sunday, although that's good, I'm talking about a true relationship with Him. You have to know what you believe and why, Fantasia. Sounds like Randall knows what he believes. For the record, is he handsome?" Ruth teased, reaching over and patting her daughter's hand.

This time Fantasia smiled. "Yes, yes, and yes! Talking about fine. Mama, he's got it going on, just like the man in my dreams."

"What man?"

"I've told you before, I've been dreaming about this guy. He's handsome, tall and definitely has it going on. In my dream it's like we are so in love with each other. I can never quite see his face but it's like I know that he is fine! You know how dreams are. Anyway, I've had the dream at least three or four times."

"Pay attention to your dreams, honey. Sometimes God uses dreams and visions to teach us or show us something. You could very well be dreaming about your future husband. Try praying about it. Ask God to reveal to you clearly what it is he's trying to show you."

"Did you just tell *me* to pray?" Fantasia laughed again. "Me?"

"Yes, I sure did." Ruth's facial expression turned serious. "God hears. Just go to him. Talk to him like you're talking to me. I guarantee you won't be disappointed."

"Okay, Ma. But enough girl talk. Fill me in on what's been going on around here while I was in Cali."

Ruth reached out her arm awkwardly toward her daughter, opened her mouth to speak.... "It's been hec—" She stopped in midsentence, grabbed hold of her right arm, squinted her eyes like she was in pain and fell back in the chair.

"Ma, are you all right?" Fantasia jumped up from her chair and rushed from behind her desk to her mother's side. "Mama, are you okay?" She watched in horror as her mother's eyes rolled back in her head.

Ruth moaned loudly, placed her right hand over her chest before she fell out of the chair and onto the floor, unconscious.

18

"Doubt is a pain too lonely to know that faith is his twin brother." Khalil Gibran

Fantasia, her siblings, and Moses gathered in the hospital's Critical Care Unit where Ruth had been since she suffered a massive heart attack several days ago when she and Fantasia were in Fantasia's office talking. Now Ruth was lying in a hospital bed in grave condition.

Fantasia got up, excused herself and went outside to answer Paula's Facetime call.

"How is Aunt Ruth?" Paula asked, her brows furrowed in worry.

Fantasia paced along the concrete pavement. "She's still on a breathing tube. The doctor says it's touch and go. She had a light stroke after she had the heart attack. It doesn't look good, Paula." Fantasia broke down. The tears she'd held back since Ruth collapsed in her office streamed down her face. The more she tried to wipe them away, the more they were replaced with fresh ones.

"I can't lose my mother, Paula. I can't. What would I do without her?"

"Shhh, it's going to be all right, Tasia. You'll see. Aunt Ruth is a fighter. She's raised three small children on her own after Uncle Solumun died. She survived that terrible car wreck when we were both teens, and she's a breast cancer survivor. Do you think something like a heart attack is going to take her out? I don't think so."

Fantasia remained quiet, briefly holding the phone next to her side.

"Fantasia, I can't see you," Paula said.

"I don't know. She looks so weak, Paula. If you saw her lying in that bed. She looks so helpless." Fantasia continued crying.

"Come on, now. You've got to pull yourself together. Our church is praying for her. She's going to make it. You just wait and see."

"Thanks, Paula. Look, I better get back inside. I'll try to call you tomorrow."

"Okay. Oh, I forgot to tell you that Randall has been asking about you and Aunt Ruth. He's genuinely concerned. He wanted me to tell you that he's praying for her to make a full recovery. He said he had tried calling and texting you."

Fantasia hesitated before answering. "Yeah, I saw his text messages. I may not be a praying person, but I'm thankful for the show of love and concern from so many people, including him. And to let you know, I haven't replied to any of my messages. All of my time and attention has been on my mother."

"He cares more about you than you think, Fantasia. You just won't give the man a fighting chance."

"Look, I don't have time to talk about Randall and his feelings. I need to get back inside." Fantasia started walking until she reached the automatic doors. "We'll talk later."

"Okay. I love you. And give Aunt Ruth a kiss from me, Nick and the girls. Tell my cousins hello."

"I will. Bye."

"Buh-bye," Paula replied as they ended their Facetime call.

Fantasia placed her phone inside her right pant pocket. Just as she went through the automatic doors and before she could make it back to the Critical Care Unit, it started ringing. She removed it from her pant pocket, looked at it, and a look of surprise filled her face. This time she answered.

"Hi," she said.

"Hi. I hope you don't mind me calling. I just want to see how your mother is doing," Randall said.

Fantasia's heart went soft. To hear Randall's voice automatically gave her a soothing sensation. She felt a calmness come over her as he spoke reassuring words of comfort and concern.

"Did you get any of my messages?"

"Yes, I did. And I'm sorry I didn't respond. I've been with my family and trying to stay by my mother's side as much as possible."

"I understand. I just wanted you to know that you have a friend in me, Fantasia. And whether you like it or not, I'm praying for your mother and your family."

"Thank you, Randall."

"No thanks necessary, but you're welcome. Did Paula happen to tell you where I am?"

"Uh, no. But I assume that you're in Cali."

"Actually, I'm not that far from you. I'm in New York."

Fantasia leaned against the building. Had she heard him correctly? Did he just say that he was in New York?

"New York?" *Business*, Fantasia immediately reasoned in her thoughts.

"Yes, that's right. New York."

"Ummm. Paula didn't mention it."

"Then she probably doesn't know. Nick probably didn't tell her. I'm here for business, but to be honest there's some family business I must take care of while I'm here. Someone I've been putting off meeting for a long time. Seems I always found a way not to come here. But I guess God had different plans, ya know."

Randall's parents and sister were deceased. So what did he mean he was in New York on family business? Fantasia didn't know what to make of it.

"So you do have other family, that's good to know."

"Yes, I normally say that I don't have family, but I came to realize that no matter whether I ever see, here, or speak to him or not, the fact remains, I have an uncle. I have family. I have never met him; never got a chance to know him or have a relationship of any kind with him. He and my father had different mothers. They didn't grow up together, so unfortunately they weren't close as brothers being that they lived on opposite ends of the country. And he's, I believe, about eleven or twelve years older than my father. He has dementia and terminal cancer. He wants to meet his brother's surviving child and only son before he dies.

"I'm glad you're going to give him his wish. How long do you plan on being in New York?"

"A few days."

Fantasia smiled. She was glad that Randall couldn't see her. "Thank you for your prayers and for calling, especially when you have your own family issues. I really appreciate it."

To Randall, hearing her voice induced a sense of calm in him, too. He couldn't shake her off for some reason. But she didn't have or desire a relationship with God. That was something that weighed heavily on Randall's mind. Could they even have a relationship when their spiritual beliefs were so far apart – so different?

"If my research is correct, I'm just a few hours from Belleaf. I can catch the train and come there."

"Come here, to Belleaf?" Fantasia shook her head slightly like she was trying to make herself wake up. Was she having another one of those crazy dreams?

"Look, if you say no, it's cool. I just thought that I would try to get there to see you before I pushed back out to Cali, you know."

"I mean, that's nice of you, but you don't have to do that."

"Fantasia."

"Yes?"

"I want to. I'll rent a car when I get there and come to the hospital or wherever you are. I'll feel better if I can see that you're taking care of yourself," he added.

"You don't have to do that, Randall. You're in New York for your family. Family always comes first, no matter if you have never laid eyes on them."

"I think I'm seeing that. A little more every day. So, look, I'll give you a call or text you when I'm leaving New York."

"Okay, I think I would enjoy seeing someone from home. Even if it is you." She quickly laughed and Randall followed suit.

He recalled a passage of scripture about laughter and thought, *A joyful heart is good medicine.*

They ended their call and Fantasia turned around for the third time to go back inside the hospital. This time, there was a smile across her face. She felt a sense of anticipation at the thought of Randall's upcoming visit, and like everything really was going to be all right, and her mother was going to be absolutely fine. She just knew it. Opening the door to Critical Care, she mouthed, "Thank you, Go—" but quickly stopped herself, shook her head, walked back inside Critical Care and rejoined the comfort of family.

19

"Faith is the bird that sings when the dawn is still dark." Rabindranath Tagore

Fantasia sat across the table from Randall, staring intently into his enchanting eyes.

"I'm glad to hear that your mother is getting better."

"Yes, hearing the doctor tell me and the rest of the family earlier today that she's being moved to a regular room was such good news. If all continues to go well, which he says he doesn't see any reason that it shouldn't, she should be able to go home in a few days."

Randall caressed Fantasia's hand, and to his surprise she didn't pull back.

"I can't thank you enough for coming. You know you really didn't have to make a detour and come to Belleaf."

"I told you; I wanted to lay eyes on you for myself, just to make sure you were hanging in there. Plus, I wanted to see your mother, say a prayer for her and your family. That's what life is all about, at least for me it is. Showing care and concern for others."

"Well, I'll be the first to admit that I believe your prayers worked, along with all the prayers and well wishes from my mother's friends and church family."

Randall eased back in his chair and appeared pleasantly surprised. "You? Admitting that prayer works? Wow, I don't know what to say to that."

Fantasia laughed and Randall smiled, taking in her beauty.

"So you act like I'm some grouchy mean person who hates any and everything that has to do with religion."

Randall said nothing.

"So you really see me like that?"

"You're not mean at all. Ummm, grouchy. Sometimes." He laughed. "As for hate, well that's such a strong word. I don't think you have a hateful bone in your body."

"I've had my reasons for believing the way that I have. When my father died, it was the most painful thing I ever went through. I remember my father dragging us off to church at least three times a week. He was always teaching us about God and I had no problem believing whatever he said and whatever the preacher said. But then out of the blue, he just collapsed in the kitchen floor and died right there. I saw it. At that very moment, all I felt was anger, anger at a God who would do this to us. My mother was distraught, her heart broken. She grieved for my daddy for years."

"I'm sorry that you went through that. And I feel you. When my family was killed, think of how I felt. One moment I was surrounded in love and the next I was left all alone. I had no one to rely on. Both my mother and father came from small families, so when they died, it was like I was left here on this earth all alone. It hurt so bad, still does."

"How did you keep from turning your back on God?"

"Who says I didn't? I was more than angry; I was pissed.

"I don't understand. From the first time I met you, you were talking God this and God that. You acted like you were the happiest man on earth."

"I wasn't always like that. I had to get to that point. Like you, my parents raised me and my sister up in the church. We went at least three times a week and twice on Sundays. But after they died, I went into a deep, dark place. I became depressed, wanted to give up on life. I was bitter toward God."

"So what changed for you?"

"I guess I got tired of living like I was the one that died. I thought about my parents and how they lived their life. They were the best parents a guy could have. They had faith and they showed it throughout my life. I began to think about how they wouldn't want me to turn my back on God, my faith, and my life. Neither would my sister. She loved writing songs for the Lord, as she would describe it. She was so kind. Slowly, and I mean slowly, I began to live. I started praying again. I remembered that my father used to tell us that a true sign of having faith in God is believing that He can even when He doesn't."

This time it was Fantasia who reached over and took hold of Randall's hand. She looked into his eyes without saying one word.

"Dessert?" the server asked as he walked up to the table.

"No, not for me," Fantasia answered.

"None for me either," replied Randall. "You can get the check please."

"How did everything go with your father's half-brother?"

"It was awkward at first, but I'm glad I had the opportunity to meet him and his wife. They're really nice people. His wife told me that they had prayed that they would be able to find me before they went to be with the Lord."

"How did they find you?" asked Fantasia.

Randall gave her a side look. "Facebook."

"That makes sense," Fantasia remarked as they walked out of the restaurant located across the street from Randall's hotel.

"What's crazy about that is I just got on social media less than a year ago."

"Are you serious?"

"Yep. I never was one into the social media stuff, but Nick convinced me that it would be a good idea, especially from a marketing perspective. So I opened Facebook, Instagram and Twitter accounts Can you believe it?"

"That *is* crazy. I'm surprised you aren't on Periscope."

"Who says that I'm not." The two of them laughed.

"Thanks for dinner," Fantasia told him as he followed her to her car. "I guess I'll head back over to see my mom."

"Since I'll be leaving tomorrow, I'd like to visit her again, say another prayer with her, if you don't mind."

"I think she would like that."

"I'm going to go to my hotel room and take a short nap. I'll text you when I'm on my way to the hospital."

"Okay. Oh, were you serious about wanting to take a tour of Trinity Three?" she asked. "It's where everything starts."

"Yes, I was serious, but you don't have time for that. Your mom comes first. I can visit your gallery another time. It'll give me an excuse to come back to Belleaf," he said, opening her car door for her.

"You don't need an excuse. Anyway, I need to leave. I'll see you in a couple of hours," she said.

"Sure thing."

As she prepared to get in the car, Randall gently tugged at her elbow. She stopped, then turned and looked at him. He kissed her lightly on her lips.

"I'll see you later," Fantasia said.

Randall turned and walked away. Fantasia started her car. As she drove out of the restaurant parking lot, she spotted Randall as he disappeared inside the hotel.

She touched her lips, smiled and drove down the street.

20

"Faith is not about everything turning out okay; faith is about being okay no matter how things turn out." Unknown

"We thank you, Lord for your healing. We thank you for hearing and answering our prayers... Amen," Randall said followed by Fantasia, Ruth, Moses and Fantasia's sister, Hope, and brother in-law, David. Her brother, Prodigal had left to fly back home earlier that day.

"Thank you for coming to see me. And thank you for your prayers," Ruth told Randall.

Ruth looked over at Fantasia with weak eyes and said, "He's a kee...kee...per. I like him," she stuttered. Her speech was slightly slurred due to the stroke, but still understandable. "You like him?" she turned slowly and looked at Moses.

Moses smiled and nodded.

"Mama?" Fantasia shook her head, smiled and then shyly looked over at Randall. "Never mind."

"I know you're going to continue to get better," Randall told Ruth. "Just keep the faith."

"Thank you. I will."

"When are you headed back to the West Coast?" Moses asked.

"Tomorrow, which is why I wanted to come by here one more time before I left. I know I won't be able to get here tomorrow."

"God bless you, young man," Moses told him.

"God bless you all too." Randall sighed. "Well, I'm going to get out of here and let you get your rest," Randall said. "It was so good to meet you, even though it was under these circumstances." He leaned in and gave Ruth a light hug before he turned and said his goodbyes to the rest of Fantasia's family.

"I guess you can tell that my mother likes you. She likes you a lot," Fantasia said as they walked along the hospital corridor.

"And I like her. She's a sweet lady. I see where you get it from."

Fantasia rolled her eyes up in her head. "Okay. Thanks," she said.

"Why did you say it like that? You act like you don't believe me."

"I'm just saying that just because my mother likes you, don't read anything into it."

"You're one tough lady. You know that."

They laughed again, something they found easy to do around each other.

"Would you like to go have a cup of coffee before we call it a night? There's a bistro in the lobby of my hotel or we can go back to the restaurant we went to for dinner that's across the street from my hotel."

"Either is cool, or if you still want to take that tour of Trinity Three, we can have coffee there. I have the best espresso maker. And I can make a mean cappuccino or mocha. Take your pick. You'll think you're at Starbucks."

"Are you sure about that?" he asked.

"Very," she said.

"Let's do it then," Randall responded.

"This place is amazing. And the art is like none I've ever seen."

"This is my dream. It feels good to be able to do what I love most in the world," she said.

They walked through the massive gallery, and upon finishing up the tour, Fantasia led him to her private upstairs apartment.

"This is niice," Randall told her as they stepped off the elevator and directly into the space. He looked around while Fantasia told him to make himself comfortable while she kicked off her shoes and headed toward the bar.

"What would you like?"

He raised his eyebrows and smiled.

"To drink?" she said, smiling back. "Cappuccino, mocha or something else?"

"Are you making fun of me?" he said, walking up on her and hypnotizing her with his eyes.

"Me?" She pointed at herself. "How could you accuse me of such a thing?" She smiled while stepping behind the bar.

"I'll have a glass of wine."

"Ahhh, Church boy, you are full of surprises." She poured both of them a glass of Red Moscato and walked from behind the bar.

Randall took both glasses and walked toward the tobacco leather sofa. He paused, looked over his shoulder, making sure she was following him. She was.

She sat down on the sofa and Randall passed her the glass of wine, then sat down next to her. She was intoxicating but he maintained his self-control.

His cell phone rang. He pulled it out of his pocket and held the phone up toward his mouth "STOP," he said. The phone stopped ringing.

"You could have taken it. Don't ignore her because of me," Fantasia said curtly.

Randall drank some of his wine, and the phone rang again.

"Why don't you answer it," Fantasia said as she took a sip of her wine followed by another sip.

"STOP," he said into the phone again.

"That can wait. I'm more interested in the person sitting next to me." He turned the phone off and leaned over slightly and sat his wine glass on the table next to the sofa then returned his attention to Fantasia. He gently removed her glass of wine from her hands.

Fantasia sat motionless.

Randall didn't hesitate. He leaned in and kissed her. First, softly but then with passion. Pushing her back on the sofa, he continued kissing her and she kissed him back.

This time there was no retreating. The heat between them was obvious. He stood up and took hold of her hand.

She led him to her bedroom and closed the door behind them.

21

"Love—It's an unexplainable feeling, an expression. Once you feel it, it's like no other thing in the world."
Snoop Dogg

Fantasia was a different person, at least that's what Ruth told her. Ruth had made a miraculous and speedy recovery and was out of the hospital. Doctors had placed a stent in her heart to help prevent blockages. She was almost back to her normal self. She was eating healthier and exercising more.

Fantasia talked to Randall at least once a day since he returned to California about three weeks prior. The evening before he left Belleaf, they had made love over and over. She would never admit that she was crazy about him, but she was. She would be flying back to California at the end of the week. She had talked to her mother about making California more like her main residence instead of Belleaf. Ruth was all for it. She wanted Fantasia to be happy and she felt like Randall might be the perfect guy for her daughter. If it took Fantasia moving to California for the chance of her being happy and falling in love, she was going to do everything she could to help her make the move.

Trinity Three was already a thriving gallery. It didn't require Fantasia being there twenty four seven, which had already been proven some time ago. Fantasia had a committed, dedicated and very capable staff.

To help make her decision easier, Ruth told Fantasia that she would come to California and stay a few weeks. Moses was willing to come too, seeing that he was stepping down as his company's COO. He was still going to be an active part of the company he had built, but as a consultant instead. He wanted to spend more time with his wife. Her heart attack gave both of them a wakeup call. They talked extensively about how fragile and quick life is. They vowed to spend more time doing what they loved, traveling, and enjoying life. Moses suggested they start looking for a vacation home in California. Ruth readily agreed.

Life was looking up!

22

"Being deeply loved by someone gives you strength, while loving someone deeply gives you courage." Lao Tzu

"I'd like to know if you would go to church with me," Randall whispered in Fantasia's ear as they snuggled in the middle of his bed.

"We just got threw fornicating and you want to ask a sista to go to church?" Fantasia rolled from under Randall, resting herself on her elbow. "Boy, you are so funny." She laughed.

"So, is that a yes?" he asked as he kissed her, pushing her back down on the bed.

"I can't..." she said while he kissed.

"I won't let you up until you say yes," he told her jokingly while continuing to smother her with kisses.

"Ummm, I like that idea," Fantasia mouthed as they made love again.

♥

"I'm glad you're here. I couldn't do this without you." Fantasia and Paula went from one boutique to the next, searching for The Dress that she was going to wear to church. She hadn't set foot inside a church since her father's funeral, so this was going to be tough.

"You're not going to walk the red carpet, Fantasia. I don't even know why we're out here shopping like you're going to the Oscars."

"I might as well be. It's not every day a girl goes to the Oscars and for this girl, it's not every day she goes to church."

"You are one crazy chick."

"I know. You tell me that every chance you get," Fantasia replied as she finally decided on a simple black A-line dress with a fitted waist and sweetheart neckline with quarter length sleeves.

The following Sunday when she walked into the church with Randall, contrary to what she thought, she felt peaceful, like she was where she belonged.

Randall held on to her hand as they walked along the church aisle, stopping at the middle row of the church and taking a seat on the soft, cloth pews.

For the next hour and a half, Fantasia reminisced about how her parents used to bring her, Prodigal and Hope to church Sunday after Sunday. Listening to the choir sing and the pastor's message about unconditional love reawakened something within and instead of feeling that she would dread being in church, she welcomed it.

The relationship she shared with Randall was like none she'd ever experienced. The more time they spent together, the more she wanted to spend with him. She found herself laughing more and stressing less.

The NT Stores were flourishing and provided Randall with a hefty income. A few months after he met his uncle, he passed away. To his surprise, his uncle left him a six figure inheritance. It wasn't until he was contacted by his uncle's attorney that he learned that he had made millions from investments and from an App he had designed for Androids.

♥

After church, Randall and Fantasia had lunch at one of her favorite restaurants before they returned to her house.

"Thank you for going to church with me today," Randall told Fantasia as they relaxed in the family room.

"It wasn't so bad. I must admit that I enjoyed it. Instead of bringing back sad memories, it made me feel like I was connected to my father. He loved church and God so much. Today, I realized how much I missed him, but I don't know how to explain it – sitting on that pew it felt like he was sitting right next to me."

"Do you think you would consider going back with me sometimes?"

"Ummm maybe. But I don't want to think about that now. Okay?"

"Sure," Randall replied before pulling Fantasia on to his lap.

Randall's phone rang, interrupting their make out session. He pulled it from off of his side, glanced at it and then turned it back on its holder without answering it.

"Why didn't you answer it? Was that your girlfriend?" Fantasia remarked with light humor resonating in her delicate voice.

"How could that be my girlfriend when I'm holding her in my arms."

"Nice answer," Fantasia said, laughing.

"Hey, I've got something I want to share with you."

"What is it?"

"Nick and I are expanding the business."

"Other than the one you're opening in New York?"

"Yeah. You know Nick has been traveling back and forth to Dubai. Things are looking great there, so we're working on a deal to open a store there."

Fantasia kissed Randall. "That's super. I'm so happy for you two."

"That means I'll have to make some trips over there."

"That's good. Maybe I can go to Dubai with you sometimes. I purchase a great deal of art from over there."

Randall's phone rang again.

"Answer the phone," Fantasia told him as she slid off his lap and stood up. "I'll make you a cappuccino while you talk. How's that?"

"Cool," Randall said as the phone continued to ring. By the time he pushed the Answer button the phone had stopped ringing, only to start ringing again.

It was one of the employees from the store. While Randall listened to the employee's complaints, his eyes didn't waver off of Fantasia. He smiled as he watched her making his cappuccino.

God, I hear you, loud and clear. He said to himself.

23

"Sometimes you can't explain what you see in a person. It's just the way they take you to a place where no one else can." Unknown

"Have a safe trip," Fantasia told Randall as she stood beside her car outside the airport terminal.

The couple kissed and embraced.

"I'll see you at the end of the week," he told her.

Driving off, Fantasia thought about how happy she was since she and Randall had officially decided they wanted a relationship. At first, it wasn't easy for her to make the choice to have a man in her life in a committed relationship. But so much had changed in her life since Randall Hughes waltzed in, and most of it was for the good. He kept her smiling on the inside and out. Her mother, sister and brother were equally ecstatic for her. She felt like she had it all, a good life, a successful career and a man who she might even be falling in love with.

They hadn't said the words 'I love you' to each other. There were a few times when Randall tried to tell her but she always stopped him either by placing her fingertips over his mouth or planting a kiss on his lips, blocking the words from coming. The idea that she could be in love terrified Fantasia.

Randall had been gone for two days, when Fantasia decided she wanted to do something to surprise him for his birthday which was only a couple of weeks away. She spent most of the day on the phone checking out venues where she could have the party until Paula convinced her that her home would be the perfect setting.

Being that Randall was not a flashy type of man, having a party at a hotel wasn't what she wanted to do. She wanted a small, intimate gathering of his closest acquaintances from work and church. Of course Paula and Nick would be there, too.

Knock. Knock.

"Yes," Fantasia asked of the person knocking on the door of her home office.

"Ms. Runsome," Bianca said."

"Come in, Bianca."

Bianca slowly turned the knob. Opening the door, she walked inside cautiously, looking like she was expecting to see something she shouldn't.

"Hey, there. How are you?" Fantasia asked.

"I...I'm not so good."

Fantasia stopped working on the details of Randall's party and looked at Bianca. "What is it, Bianca? Are you not feeling well? Are the kids okay?"

"I have something to show you. I don't think you will like it," she said in broken English. When Bianca was upset or excited her Spanish accent was especially thick. Today was such an occasion.

"Sit down. You look like you just saw a ghost. Tell me, what's wrong?"

"I saw Mr. Randall today." Bianca responded without making a move to sit down.

Fantasia giggled. "No, you couldn't have, Bianca. He's out of town until Friday, another two days."

"No, I'm sure it was him."

Fantasia looked amused. Bianca seemed to have it set in her mind that she saw Randall.

"Bianca, I'm telling you, Randall is out of town."

"I must show you something?" Bianca asked, walking up to Fantasia's desk, while scrolling through her cell phone.

"Sure, let's see what you have there."

"Promise you won't fire me," Bianca said tearfully.

"Fire you? Bianca, what on earth is wrong with you. Why would I fire you? Come on, show me."

Bianca scrolled until she found what she was searching for in her phone, then passed the device to Fantasia.

Fantasia began watching the video. Were her eyes deceiving her? No, it couldn't be, but it was. Randall. Bianca knew what she was talking about.

"Oh my gosh," Fantasia screamed, throwing one hand over her mouth then looking up at Bianca who looked terrified.

"I'm sorry, Ms. Runsome. But I told you. It is Mr. Hughes."

"Not only was it Randall with his arm around the waist of a woman, the woman was Hilary! They were walking out of a restaurant looking like the perfect couple.

Fantasia inhaled then exhaled. Passing the phone back to Bianca, she looked faint. "Bianca, how long ago was this?"

"About an hour ago."

"Whatever you do, please do not delete that video. Text it to me."

"Yes, ma'am."

"If you'll leave me alone, I would appreciate it."

"Are you going to be okay?"

"I'm fine, just fine."

Bianca walked away. Before exiting Fantasia's office, she looked over her shoulder as if she wanted confirmation that Fantasia would be fine.

"I'm good," Bianca. "Please, just go."

Bianca left the office, closing the door behind her.

Fantasia reached for her bag off the table behind her, ran out of her office, down the hall, and didn't stop until she reached the garage.

She climbed in her SUV and drove until she arrived at Randall's complex. Drawing in a nervous breath, she pulled up to the gated community and put in the code Randall had recently shared with her.

After finding a parking space, she sat inside her vehicle for several minutes. Randall had a private garage so she had no way of knowing if he was at home or not. She stepped outside her vehicle and boldly walked up to his door.

One thought after another filtered through her mind until she could hardly take anymore.

Ring. Ring. Ring. She pushed the doorbell.

"Uh, hello," Hilary said as she cracked open the door barely wide enough for Fantasia to see her face.

"Hilary, is that you?" Fantasia asked.

"Randall's not here," she immediately told Fantasia.

♥

"Open this door," Fantasia ordered.

"What do you want?" Hilary asked, opening the door a little wider enabling Fantasia to see her swollen tummy.

"You're pregnant?" Fantasia screamed.

"Yes, *we* are," Hilary answered smugly, carefully placing one hand on her tummy.

"Where is Randall?"

"Hilary," Fantasia heard Randall call out.

"I'm coming, sweetheart," replied Hilary, looking back over her shoulder and then back at Fantasia.

"Look, I'm sorry, sweetie, but Randy is taking a shower. Do you mind calling him later? We just got here a few minutes ago and we have plans. I'm sure whatever business you're here about can wait," she said mockingly without taking her eyes off Fantasia.

"I'm not the one to play with, Hilary." Fantasia pushed the door open and forced her way inside. Hilary ran from the door.

Randall appeared, his body glistening from the shower, and with a white towel wrapped around his chiseled lower body. He stopped when he saw Fantasia standing inside the apartment.

"Did I hear you talking to someone at the d— Fantasia? What... what are you doing here?"

"What am *I* doing here? What is *she* doing here? Better yet, what are *you* doing here? You're a long way from New York. You lying, cheating bastard!"

Hilary stood to the side, a pleasant smirk on her face.

"She busted in," Hilary spoke up like she was about to cry. "I tried to stop her. I thought you said she was nothing to you."

"Be quiet, Hilary!" Randall yelled. "Fantasia, it's not what you think. I swear it isn't."

"So now you've resulted to swearing, huh... and lying."

Fantasia turned to walk back out of the apartment.

Randall ran toward her, but Fantasia shut the door as hard as she could. Running toward her SUV, she heard Randall calling out her name, but she didn't stop until she made it to the vehicle.

Climbing inside, she sped off, blinded by tears.

24

"Trusting you is my decision. Proving me right is your choice." Unknown

Randall left message after message and text after text, but Fantasia refused to answer any of them. She listened to his countless voicemails and read his texts, but it only made her angrier. Randall had proven to be a liar and a cheat, and she hated herself for falling for him in the first place.

"Fantasia, how many times do I have to tell you that I didn't know she was coming here. She surprised me at the store, telling me that she flew in for a convention with her job. She had some free time and so we did have lunch. She even told me that she had met someone and was pregnant with his kid."

Fantasia sat in her bedroom chair, listening to the message.

Her phone rang. It was Paula. They exchanged their usual banter before Paula asked her what the latest news was on Randall.

"I just listened to his sorry voicemail again. He really wants me to believe that the reason she was at his apartment is because she wanted to talk about the dude she's pregnant by."

"Yeah you told me that the supposedly baby daddy told Hilary that the baby isn't his. That's wild," Paula said, "but what did she expect. These guys ain't loyal."

"I know right. That's why she needed someone to talk to and he had to be Mr. Captain

Save uh...girl, don't let me get started on Randall Hughes. I'm done."

"I think he's telling the truth," Paula responded. "You said he had just flown in from New York when everything went down. He was planning on surprising you, hoping you two would celebrate him closing the deal early on the New York stores. Nick is so excited, girl, so you know Randall is too."

"Did you hear anything I said?" Fantasia rolled her eyes. "And he expects me to believe that foolery?"

"Look, you know how conniving we females can be, especially when we can't get what we want, Fantasia. I mean, I really do think he's telling the truth. From the screenshots of the texts you sent me from him, and listening to the voicemail messages, I believe him. I even talked to Nick and he says the same thing. Hilary messed up their relationship and she's trying anything she can to get back with him, but it's not working. She's playing on his sympathy, probably praying that he feels so sorry for her and her unborn child, that he'll take her back. Crazy broad. He loves you. I just know that he does."

"You know more than I do then. Here I was going to church with that bum. What in the world was I thinking? How could I have been so stupid?"

"You're in love, not stupid, so stop saying that you are."

"No, you got that wrong. I'm not in love, not at all. Anyway, that's enough of that. I'm flying back to Belleaf one day this week. I've got to get away from here. Clear my head, you know."

"It's time for you to stop running, Fantasia. Face the problem head on. Any relationship takes hard work, trust and communication. I'm not saying that Randall is perfect because he isn't. He's far from perfect, but so are you. At least talk to the man before you go running away like a little girl."

"Me, a little girl, I'm far from that. I can handle my own."

"Maybe you can, but we're not talking about handling your own, like you handle your business. I'm talking about can you handle your heart by forgiving. He messed up, but did he mess up so bad that you can't forgive him?"

Night after night, Fantasia's dreams haunted her. What once were sensual, romantic dreams about her mystery man had turned into dreams of her and Randall. Normally, she would have welcomed them, but dreaming about him making love to her, them running off across the fields like some hyped up television commercial, was getting next to her. There was another dream where she saw herself standing on the top of a mountain. She was crying because Randall was about to fall off a cliff. She couldn't reach him in time to save him. She woke up in a cold sweat. Why wouldn't he leave her alone? Why did he torment her even in her dreams?

Over and over again, she listened to the last message that he had left.

"Fantasia, I'm sorry for hurting you. I'm sorry for destroying the trust you had in me. But please

believe me when I say that nothing happened between Hilary and me. I promise you that it didn't. I wish you would forgive me. Believe me. Give me another chance to prove to you that I love you, Fantasia. I really, really love you."

25

"If life can remove someone you never dreamed of losing; it can replace them with someone you never dreamt of having." Rachel Wolchin

Fantasia fell back into her normal routine, throwing herself into her work. During the two months since she returned to Belleaf, she had finalized the details for opening the art center in Broknfield, and chosen a developer for the galleries she was opening in Cali. Things at Trinity Three were busier than ever and she and Ruth were about to host one of the largest art events in Washington.

Randall had finally stopped calling and texting. From what Paula told her, like Fantasia, he had poured himself into his work. Paula said he had become a workaholic so much so that Nick rarely had to handle many of the business dealings because Randall was on top of everything.

Nick told her that Randall was still in love with Fantasia. Nick said that he told Hilary that he didn't want her to ever contact him again after what she had done.

Paula listened as Nick told her about the life changing decision Randall had made. She couldn't wait to Facetime Fantasia to let her know.

"You know what, it's time for you to act like the grown woman you are."

"What do you mean act like a grown woman? What in the world are you talking about anyway?"

"You're about to let the best thing that ever happened to you walk out of your life all because of your stinking pride."

"Look, if you're still stuck on talking about Randall, you can take that somewhere else because I don't want to hear it. I have so moved on from that dude," Fantasia lied. "The old Fantasia is back, and she is not one to be fooled with, messed over, walked on or stepped on. So miss me with all the theatrics, Paula."

"This is far from theatrics. I'm going to tell you this one last time and if you want to continue to act stubborn and pretend like you don't love that man, then so be it. I'll leave it alone after I tell you this."

"Tell me then, so I can get back to work. I've got things to do here, girl."

"Randall is moving."

Fantasia's heart suddenly skipped a beat. "Moving? Where is he moving to? Phoenix, to be with little miss Hilary?"

"Dubai."

"Huh? Did you say Dubai?"

"Yes, I sure did. I don't stutter. Randall is moving to Dubai. He's going to manage the stores they're opening over there."

"Oh is that right? Well, I wish him well."

"Is that all you have to say? Aren't you going to call the man? Are you going to let him go that easily? What is wrong with you?"

"I can't stop him, even if I wanted to. If that's what he wants to do with his life, then so be it."

"Listen to yourself. You don't mean that. Maybe you don't realize it, but I do.... you love Randall, Fantasia."

"I don't know what makes you think that."

"I know you. We're not only blood, we're best friends. I know you inside out. And I'm telling you this, you have forty-eight hours to get your butt to California and stop that man from walking out of your life forever."

That evening, Fantasia did something she hadn't done since she arrived back in Belleaf, that was talk to her mother. Ruth knew what had gone down, that much Fantasia told her, but every time Ruth approached her to discuss the matter, Fantasia shut her out. Hearing the news that Randall was moving to Dubai pressed on her heart.

"Mama, I don't know what to do. He hurt me. He hurt me bad," Fantasia cried, her head resting on Ruth's chest.

Ruth rubbed her on the head and back as she held on to her oldest child. "Baby, from what I know about Randall, from the way he made you smile, made you laugh, I believe he is the man for you. I've been praying and praying about you and him for a long long time. I'm not saying that he didn't think more wisely when it came to that young lady, but I do know that he loves you. He's told me many times."

"He has?" Fantasia raised her head up and looked into her mother's eyes.

"Just about every time I've talked to him, he tells me that he wants me to know that he loves my daughter." Ruth grinned.

"So he messed up, we all mess up in life. Do you think Moses and I have a perfect relationship? No, we don't. But we love each other enough to work through the tough times. We refuse to give up on our love.

Baby, if you love this man, if you really love him, then don't let him leave these United States without you telling him how you feel. You can be stubborn just like your daddy, but I'm telling you that if you want to be happy, then you have to learn how to forgive, sweetie. Even if you decide that you don't want to be with him, you still need to find it in your heart to forgive that man.

I want you to think about what I'm telling you. Life is too short to walk around carrying unforgiveness in your heart."

♥

That same night, after talking to Ruth, Fantasia had another one of her dreams. This time, she saw a man with no face walking away from her. It was night time in the dream. Stars were shining brightly. She was reaching out for him but each time he was out of her reach. He kept walking along a winding path until all she could see was a silhouette of him. She could hear her name being called softly like it was being carried by the wind. She picked up her pace until she was running. She was trying to get to him before he disappeared.

Fantasia woke up and bolted upright in the middle of her bed. Sweat had formed on her forehead and hot tears streamed down her face.

She jumped out of the bed, grabbed her phone off the nightstand and made a call. "Olivia, I need you to get me the quickest flight you can find to Cali, even if you have to rent a flight. Do whatever it takes."

♥

"Man, I'm going to miss you," Nick told Randall. "I know you're going to do great in Dubai, but I'm telling you, I would much rather you stay in Cali, bro. We have capable staff in Dubai and we can continue to handle the business over there like we already do."

"Yeah, but we need a presence over there. Plus, it's nothing for me here, bro. I don't have any family to keep me here. I don't have a wife or kids and being that you do, I can relieve you of some of that traveling by setting up residence over there."

"That all sounds good, but we're in this business together. Our plans were for us to take turns going over there, not moving over there, not unless we need to later on. I just hope you've thought long and hard about this. It's not too late to change your mind, you know."

"Yeah, I know. But I think starting with a clean slate in my life will be good for me. I believed in my heart that I had met the girl for me. I prayed about me and Fantasia, but things just didn't work out. I blew it man. I really blew it. Anyway, I'm outta here. I better get inside. My flight will be leaving in a couple of hours, and I still haven't gone through TSA. You know how long that can take."

"You be safe, bro," Nick told him and then gave him a hug.

"We'll talk when you get there."

"Yeah, most definitely."

♥

Fantasia drove to Randall's apartment, rushed out of her car, and rang the doorbell. No one answered. Finally, the next door neighbor walked up. She told Fantasia that Randall had moved out several days before. Fantasia thanked the woman and then headed for the men's store. She turned into the parking lot at the same time Nick was getting out of his car.

"Hey, what are you doing here, cuz?" Nick asked.

"Where is Randall?" Fantasia asked him.

"I just dropped him off at the airport."

"Oh my God, please, God, don't let him leave," she cried out.

"Get in my car, I'll drive you there. I don't want you killing yourself."

Fantasia followed Nick's orders. All the way to the airport she prayed out loud.

Nick couldn't believe what he was hearing. Fantasia was actually praying. He prayed within himself that they would make it in time.

As soon as he drove up to the terminal, Fantasia jumped out almost before he came to a complete stop. She dashed off inside the terminal. Nick had given her the flight number and gate. Knowing that she couldn't get to the gate because of security, she had an agent to page Randall Hughes over the intercom.

"Randall Hughes, please report to the ticket agent. Randall Hughes, it is urgent that you report to the ticket counter," the agent repeated.

Five minutes...seven minutes...ten minutes. Fantasia's spirit dropped. She had missed him. Tears poured heavily down her cheeks.

"Oh, God, why, why did you let me love him only to lose him?"

"You didn't lose me."

Scared to look around, Fantasia stood grounded in the middle of the airport terminal.

"Fantasia," Randall said again. This time he reached out to her, and gently turned her around to face him.

"Randall, I'm so sorry. I was so stubborn. I should have believed you. Please, will you forgive me? Please."

Randall gathered her into his arms and held her next to him. "Shhh," he whispered as he wiped the tears from her eyes. "I'm here. I'm not going anywhere. I love you, girl."

Fantasia looked up lovingly into his piercing gray eyes. "I never knew I could feel this way. I thought love existed only in my dreams, but you made me realize that love transcends even our dreams. I love you Randall Hughes...I love you.

Thank you, God," Randall whispered.

Fantasia eased back slightly and spoke. "Yes, thank you...God.

The End

Other titles by Shelia E. Bell (also Shelia Lipsey)

YA Titles
House of Cars
The Life of Payne

Novels
Show A Little Love (*out of print*)
Always Now and Forever Love Hurts
Into Each Life
Sinsatiable
What's Blood Got To Do With It?
The Real Housewives of Adverse City (*Spring 2016*)

Series Books

Beautiful Ugly
True Beauty (*sequel to Beautiful Ugly*)

My Son's Wife Series
My Son's Wife
My Son's Ex-Wife: The Aftermath
My Son's Next Wife
My Sister My Momma My Wife
My Wife My Baby…And Him
The McCoys of Holy Rock (*Summer 2016*)

Anthologies
Bended Knees
Weary to Will
Learning to Love Me

Nonfiction
A Christian's Perspective: Journey Through Grief

Contact information
www.sheliaebell.net
sheliawritesbooks@yahoo.com
sheliawritesbooks@gmail.com
www.facebook.com/shelialipseyreaders
@sheliaebell (Twitter & Instagram)